In
memory of
Leonard Benson

1

Sometimes Eric had trouble keeping his big worry to himself. *I'm scared to tell most people,* he thought as he put the second coat of purple paint on his bike. *Like Dad. He'd be sure to tell the sheriff or a policeman. That's what ought to be done. But if Ron and those other guys found out who told— man! They'd really clobber me.*

Eric knew of only one person he could tell about what he had seen and heard that evening. *Anne won't blab what I tell her to anyone. Not unless I tell her it's okay. She's not like the sisters of some of my friends.*

As he put the one-inch paintbrush in a can of

cleaning fluid, Eric thought, *Why haven't I talked to Anne about this already? It's been nearly a week since I saw Ron and the others break out the church windows. But it seems like a year.* He remembered how he felt when he looked through the shrubbery in Mrs. Wilton's back yard that evening. He'd been mowing her grass. He had stopped, shut off the mower, and was clipping the straggles around a flower bed. Clippers didn't make much noise. *That's why no one knew I was across the alley from the church.*

First Eric heard voices, mixed together. As they came closer he could tell that Ron Cranor was in the group. He never said anything until he used the words, "Face up, you guys." Eric had figured out that this was the way Ron made sure everyone listened to him, and that he wouldn't want anyone else ever to use those same words. *It's like it's his personal thing*, Eric decided.

As Eric cleaned purple splatters from his hands he thought, *I wish I'd said, "Face up," myself once in awhile. If I had stood up to Ron maybe he wouldn't have gotten into so much meanness. Some of us wouldn't go along with his ideas, but plenty of guys did. And girls sometimes.*

All at once Eric realized why he hadn't talked to his sister about the breaking of the stained-glass windows. *It's because Buffy Standish was with Ron. Anne used to like her a lot. She felt sorry for her anyway. Anne wouldn't want to know Buffy might be in a bunch of trouble if anyone besides me*

Someone said, "A car's turning in the alley," and the others in the group ran past Eric.

finds out who threw the pieces of brick.

Eric rubbed at a splotch of paint until the skin on the back of his hand was red. *I wish I could quit thinking about what I heard and saw. It keeps going around in my head, like pictures flashing on a screen.* He remembered getting up on his knees when he heard the sound of glass breaking. He pulled down on a branch of a lilac bush in time to see Ron put his arm back and aim at a second window. Someone said, "A car's turning in the alley," and the others in the group ran past Eric. Larry Ross was first. He was always glued to Ron's side. That's how it seemed anyway. There were two boys Eric didn't know. Then came Buffy and the new girl who'd come to Somerset Middle School not long before the end of the year.

Eric remembered that he'd sat down on the grass, wishing he was in someplace else—anywhere except across the alley from the church with two broken windows. The car that had turned in the alley stopped not far from where Eric was hiding. *Only I wasn't really hiding until I saw the flashing red light. I was just there doing what I was supposed to be doing.*

Since that afternoon the same questions had bounced around in Eric's mind over and over: *Should I have walked out and told the city policeman what I saw and heard? Would he have believed me? Or would he have thought I was the brick thrower?*

Eric looked at the clock above his dad's workbench. *It's still running—after we worked on it!* He remembered selling seeds up and down the streets in Somerset. The yellow and white kitchen clock was the prize he'd chosen. When he gave it to his mother she cried a little and hugged him. "I thought you were going to get a chemistry kit—or was it a wood-burning set?" she asked.

"I changed my mind," Eric said. He knew why his mother couldn't bear to part with the clock and kept it on the wall for a long time after it quit running.

Four-thirty. I think I'll go in and see what's for supper. A brown lid danced on a cream-colored pan, and wisps of steam curled into the air. *I know what's cooking,"* Eric thought. *Chicken. Mom's probably going to have dumplings or noodles. Either's okay—double okay.*

"Eric," his mother called from the family room. "I'm down here. Do you want something?"

"Not exactly—unless you'll let me have a snack."

"Why not? We won't eat until six. And that's a long time if you're hungry. There's milk and apples in the refrigerator."

"Is Anne home?"

"Yes. She's in her room. Why don't you come in and talk to me for awhile?"

"Okay," Eric said, "after I scrub and change and get rid of the paint and turpentine smell." He passed the door of his sister's room, but didn't see her.

By the time he was ready to go downstairs Anne was at his door. "You busy?" she asked. "Too busy to talk?"

"Here? Or downstairs?"

"Here's better, for what I have on my mind," Anne said. She walked to the window, stood with her back to him, and began to talk.

11

"I'm really scared, Ric," she said. "I don't know how to begin."

Several thoughts circled in Eric's mind while he waited to hear what Anne had on her mind. He could almost hear his mother say, "I thought when I chose your name that no one would give you a nickname. Then your own sister found a way to shorten it." He also thought, *I've never seen Anne as scared as she seems now.* He sat down on his bed.

"It's about the meanness that's going on—the vandalism," Anne said as she turned, pulled out his desk chair, and sat down. "And I know Buffy's mixed up with Ron and his groupies."

"Oh?"

"The way you say *oh* makes me think you know something about this."

"Could be, depending what you mean by *this.*"

"I mean breaking the church windows and smearing ink and paint over the carpet in the library—and who knows what else."

"Well—I only know about the windows," Eric said. He took a deep breath. "That's because I saw it happen."

"You *saw* it?"

"Yes. I was in Mrs. Wilton's yard."

"Did they see *you?*" Anne asked.

"No. No one did. Not even the town marshall. I stayed behind the lilac bush where I was when I first heard Ron."

"Were you scared?"

"I sure was. But that wasn't the worst part. I thought I ought to tell someone."

"You didn't—not anyone. Were you afraid?"

"No. I wasn't afraid to *tell.* It was just—"

"I know. You were afraid that Ron would find out who told. So am I."

"Say—how do you know what that bunch of kids are doing?"

"From—but first, promise not to let anyone else know who told me. Not until the right time."

"Okay, I promise."

"Well, it was Buffy's older sister, Ruth. She's married and lives in one of those apartments over on Bundy Street." Anne explained that she'd been babysitting in the apartment building and when she started home Buffy's sister stopped her. "She knew Buffy and I used to do fun things together and she said she wished we still did."

"And her sister told you about Buffy being with Ron that day?"

"Yes. She was sure it was Ron who had influenced her sister. Buffy's got a real crush on him. When Ruth tried to talk to Buffy, Buffy admitted that she knew so much that she could never break off with Ron—not even if she wanted to—which she didn't."

"That's stupid. It sounds like slavery."

"I know," Anne said. "But it goes on. Some people make others afraid."

"Like us. We're not telling what *we* know."

"And that's not right, Ric. We know it."

"What's going on up there?" their mother called.

"We got to talking, Mom," Anne said as she went to the door. "Is it time to set the table?"

"Not quite," Eric heard his mother say.

"We'll be down anyway, a little later."

"I'm going now," Eric said. "Are we—should we tell Mom?"

"We should. I know that. And I don't dread telling her. It's what may happen afterward that's scary. I mean, it's like when things get moving and you can't stop them."

"*Are* we going to tell Mom or *aren't* we?"

"Let's get it over with," Anne said. "I can't go on knowing all this without talking about it with her and Dad."

"That's how I felt—about you."

"You *did!* You wanted to talk to me?"

"Yes. But not to anyone else. Not now anyhow."

Anne smiled and touched the back of Eric's hand with one finger. "Knowing that gives me a great feeling. Thanks."

"You're welcome, Ann with an E."

"Don't say it. You know I don't like being called Annie."

2

The telephone rang as Eric reached the bottom step. He raced Anne to the desk in the living room. She waited until he said, "It's for Mom! Aunt Lila."

"Wow! We'll never get to talk to Mom now," Anne said.

"Never's a long time, as Dad always says."

Anne had set the table and Eric had read all of the evening paper that interested him before their mother came to the kitchen. "I finally told Lila I had to get supper."

"What'd she want?"

"It took me all this time to find out. I thought she'd never get to the point."

"*What* point, Mom?"

"The speaker for our church circle—the state trooper. Now! I must drop the dumplings in the broth."

"Why are you having a trooper?" Eric asked. He leaned over the end of the cooper-colored range and watched the yellow squares of dough puff into little pillows.

"To talk about vandalism and how to protect ourselves," his mother said. "It's so sad, to me, to have to talk about *that*. We ought to be concerned with why vandalism happens."

Eric turned his head and looked at Anne. She raised her eyebrows and pointed toward the back door. *Dad's home. The truck door slammed. I guess we won't talk about the mess Buffy and Ron are in. Not right now.*

"The air's a little nippy out there," Jeremy Markely said after he'd been welcomed by his family. "It may even frost tonight."

"Oh, I'd better cover up my tomato vines after we eat. There are several to ripen yet. Don't let me forget."

"I'll do it now if there's time," Eric said.

"Thank you," his mother said. "Use the same sheets of plastic, and—"

"I know. Weight the corners with stones from around the flower beds."

It was nearly dark by the time Eric went inside. Somerset was almost as quiet as the country. A dog yapped from somewhere across the street. The rumble of a Norfolk and Western freight train was fading into the distance.

By the time the Markelys left the table, the clock

on the fireplace was chiming nine o'clock. They were eating stewed pears and chocolate bit cookies when Anne said, "Ric and I have something we want you to know."

"Does this have anything to do with the long conversation you two had earlier?" her mother asked.

"Yes. Do you want me to begin, Ric?"

"No, I will. Because I saw—what I saw." Eric took a long breath before he began to talk. When he finished he said, "I guess I deserve to be bawled out, or something."

No one said anything, so he went on. "I knew I should have told you—or someone."

"But he was afraid," Anne said. "So have I been—scared to talk. I mean kids get threatened or hurt sometimes."

"That's intimidation," Eric's mother said.

"I guess," Eric said, "but if Ron knew, he might bother us and damage our house or other things."

"Do you really think he'd dare go that far?" his father asked. "I know Ron. At least I thought I did. His dad used to come in the nursery sometimes for fruit trees, I think."

"What would he do with fruit trees? They must have moved," Anne said. "They live in a second-floor apartment. Those new ones on Fairlane. Anyway, that's what Buffy said."

"Buffy? What does she have to do with Ron?"

"Too much," Anne said. "At least that's how it seems to me."

The four Markelys looked back and tried to match the picture they had of Buffy and Ron with what Eric and Anne had seen and reported. The questions, "What happened, who's to blame, and what can be done?" were discussed in great detail.

"I'm sure the Cranors have provided a good home for Ronald," Eric's mother said. "Especially if they can afford one of those condominiums."

"Could be that's part of the problem," Jeremy Markely said. "I don't know the Cranors too well. But they may be like a lot of other parents who give their kids everything they want—even before the children know they want it. Such kids often don't appreciate much of anything. They don't respect property. Their parents spoil them rotten."

"I guess we're not in any danger of having that happen to us, Anne," Eric said. "Not with work charts and lawn mowing and babysitting, candy-striping, and everything."

"No," Anne said. "We have our time pretty much scheduled."

"Poor you. Slave drivers for parents," Jeremy Markely said.

Eric grinned. Then he asked, "But what *fun* could it be to break good stuff? We used to throw rocks at bottles in the junk. I don't know why. Maybe it seemed like fun then. Even that seems stupid now."

"Like I said," his mother continued, "we need to think about causes—not just deal with results. We should see what can be done."

"Maybe nothing can," Eric said. "But it'd be great if something could."

"Well, I refuse to accept the idea that things can't be better," his mother said. "Somehow, sometime, answers should be found."

Eric's father grinned. "Somerset doesn't know it, but changes are going to be made around here. When your mother speaks in that tone of voice things are bound to happen."

"Maybe the vandalism won't be so bad," Anne said. "With school starting next week, kids will be busier." Then she pushed her chair back and shook her head. "But things get broken there too."

Eric went to the living room and flipped the switch on the television set. He didn't pay close attention to the singer or the actors behind her. He was trying to remember something his industrial arts teacher said one day. What *was* it? It had something to do with tearing things up—with vandalism.

Then Mr. Porter's words came to him. The class was talking about someone setting fire to the covered bridge out by Plainview. A boy in the back of the room had laughed and said, "Man! That must have been a great sight. I wish I'd have been there."

Mr. Porter was writing dates on the board about when projects were to be finished. He put down the chalk, walked to his desk, and sat down on one corner. That's when Eric learned that it was Larry Ross, who had to repeat the class, who wished he could have seen the blazing bridge. He was new in Somerset then. "You think you'd like to have a car of your own sometime?" the teacher asked.

Answers like "Sure" and "Who wouldn't" and "Yeah man" came from all over the classroom.

"I'm asking Larry," Mr. Porter said.

"Well, I'd be crazy if I didn't," Larry answered.

"The point I'm getting at is this," the teacher said. "How would you like it if I set it on fire?"

"Now *that's* crazy," Larry said.

"Would that be any different from someone burning the bridge?"

19

No one answered for awhile. Eric turned and caught a glimpse of Larry's red face. He didn't have to say a word. Ron answered for him. "Face up. The bridge didn't belong to anyone."

"Didn't it? How about the people who traveled over it? And the taxpayers whose money went into it? And the men who worked to build it? It's property, owned property, just as your car would be."

No one said anything except Mr. Porter who told them to get back to their schoolwork. Eric heard Ron and Larry muttering words like *straight* and *square*. To Eric they were good words, but the tone of the boys' voices made them seem bad.

As Eric remembered that day he thought, *I guess what Mr. Porter was saying was a little like the Golden Rule.* "Do to others what you would like them to do to you, or don't do what you wouldn't want done to yourself." *Something like that. I hadn't thought about that for a long time.*

Anne came into the family room. "Fix this in your mind, little brother. I did the dishes tonight. *So* don't try to tell me tomorrow it's not your turn. Hey, want to play something? Or are you watching television?"

"No, not really. How about Scrabble? I think I could beat you left handed tonight."

Eric liked words. He didn't say much about it to anyone, partly because he had the idea boys were *supposed* to like math better. But he didn't, and sometimes wondered who did all this deciding about who's supposed to like what.

"I'm going to win big tonight," he said as he lined the wooden squares on the grooved rack.

"What makes you think *that?*"

"Because of that *little brother* tag you pinned on me. I've got to prove something—I don't know what, just something."

Eric won easily and felt better. *Not just because I won*, he thought. *But keepin my mind on making words make the talk of trouble seem far away. And that's okay by me. If it'd only stay there!*

As they stored the Scrabble squares and board Eric said, "Dad and Mom didn't say what we should do about telling who broke the church windows."

"They will," Anne said. "You know how they always do. They'll want to think on it overnight."

"Right. That means we'll have a family confabulation tomorrow."

"Confabulation? Is that a real word?"

"Sure. I looked it up. It means to talk together."

3

Eric helped his father in the nursery and greenhouse on Saturdays unless he had yards to mow. He liked parts of this job. But he didn't enjoy spading around small trees and clumps and bringing up the ball of roots and earth. His back ached from bending and he'd learned that the sharp edge of the spade cut through the soles of sneakers. He kept a pair of worn clodhoppers under the counter in the salesroom.

"What are we going to do today?" Eric asked as he ate the last of his bowl of cereal.

"A lot of business, I hope," his father said. "I have a Norway pine and four flowering crabs to deliver. But I have some jobs for you to do. I think I'll have you transplant chrysanthemums from the beds into clay pots, besides waiting on customers while I'm out."

"Great. I enjoy doing that," Eric said. He liked the feel of the moist and mealy potting soil, the spicy smell of the plants, and the many colors of their flowers—rust, lilac, yellow, white, and gold.

"I was thinking," Eric's mother said. "If you don't work too late, could we go to the park tonight? There's a band concert. Anyone interested?"

"Not in the concert," Anne said. "But I'd like to go canoeing on the lake—if you'll help me row, Dad."

"I'm willing, so let's plan that way. Could we have a picnic maybe? We'll be home no later than five-thirty."

As Eric worked, he thought of Ron and how his vandalism was affecting others, people like Buffy and Larry and those whose things had been broken. *And it affects me and Anne and Buffy's sister and all the people who are worried.* He looked up and around at the many panes of glass that made up the walls and ceiling of the greenhouse. *If Ron got mad at me, he'd sure have a lot of glass to break.*

Mr. Porter, the industrial arts teacher, was one of the customers who came while Eric's father was delivering trees. "You the boss here?" he asked as he came down the aisle between the tables of plants.

"No, not really. But my dad will be back soon if I can't get what you want."

"You probably can. My wife's been hoping I'd catch the hint when she talked about a hanging basket she saw over here. It had Swedish ivy in it."

"It's above the table near the back in the next aisle. There are five or six sizes."

"I'll look and choose one," Mr. Porter said. "You go on with what you're doing."

As Eric gave the teacher change from a ten-dollar bill his father came through the door. "Getting good service from my assistant?"

"Couldn't expect better. Got what I came for and the right change. No kicks."

"While you're here, do you have a minute or two to spare?"

"More if more's needed," Mr. Porter said.

"Well—Eric's mother and I meant to talk to *him* about this before calling you, but since you're here I might as well let you turn an idea over in your mind."

This is about Ron. I know. Eric started back to the potting bench.

"Don't go," his father said. "I want you to hear." He set his blue denim hat back on his head and plunged into the subject of vandalism. "Our kids talked to us last night about something they know. I'll not go into that until we've talked as a family. But Ellen brought up the idea of calling concerned people together. We'd see if anyone could come up with a—well maybe, a solution's too much to hope for—with a way of cutting down on the problem."

"I qualify as a concerned citizen," Mr. Porter

Mr. Porter, the industrial arts teacher, was one
of the customers who came while Eric's
father was delivering trees.

said. "At least I think so. But how'd you know that?"

"No mystery about it. Eric, here, has told me about your positive stands in class."

Mr. Porter grinned and said, "I gave myself away, huh?"

"Yes," Eric said. "Mainly when you talked about the burning bridge."

"The point is this," Jeremy Markely said. "If we call a meeting, could you come?"

"I could, and I can think of some others who would likely come too."

"Fine. You'll hear from us."

After the teacher left and his father went to the lots where the young trees grew, Eric thought about what might happen. *Even if grown-ups want to do the right things, kids don't always see it the same way.* He remembered when his cousin Melanie's best friend was taking drugs. She'd been in real trouble and had to be in the hospital. Even after that she told Melanie she was sixteen and old enough to make up her own mind. *I think Melanie gave her a great answer. She told her that being a certain age doesn't mean you're smart enough to make the right decisions. But that girl probably didn't listen. I don't know what ever happened to her. She went away and I never heard where.*

Eric's father went to a drive-in restaurant for cheeseburgers, milkshakes, and apple turnovers. They ate outside the side door, close enough to hear the bell which clanged when anyone came in the salesroom.

"Tired, Eric?"

"No. Not much anyway."

26

"Well, I am. But it's not a bad feeling. It's good to know that what we worked to grow and bent to dig will make places look better. But we may not be as busy this afternoon. You could go on home."

"No, I'd rather stay."

By closing time Eric had transplanted over one hundred clumps of flowers. He knew his father was going to advertise a sale for the next weekend. *This many will give him a headstart.*

The sun was almost hidden behind the rim of trees on the horizon when the Markelys reached the park outside the city on the state highway. They ate from a picnic table on the crest of a rolling hill. Eric could see the rusting cannon across the valley on another slope. Down below, ducks and geese and swans moved slowly on the lake like boats from long ago. Their heads were like the carved prows he'd seen in history books.

Anne brought up the subject of what should be done about telling who broke the church windows. She slipped a tuna fish sandwich from a plastic bag and asked, "Have you decided? Who should we tell?"

"We haven't—not until we know what you think should be done," her mother said.

"I already *know* that," Eric said. "It's what comes afterward that scares me."

"But that's a burden that you shouldn't have to bear," his mother said. "The law or parents should share."

"I don't know, Mom," Anne said. "Kids like Ron don't pay much attention to the law or parents. And who knows, maybe parents don't care much either. Buffy's don't, I know. She told me once that she feels in the way. Her mother told her that they'd rent her room once she wasn't underfoot."

"Are you sure about this?" Ellen Markely asked.

"That's what Buffy said. Lots of times."

She probably follows Ron and the others because they make her feel wanted, Eric thought.

Before the picnic basket was repacked the Markelys had reached a decision. Eric's father led into it by saying, "I have an idea. I don't know why I didn't think of it before. How about asking advice from Jim Sheffield?"

"Of course! Why didn't we think of him? Would you feel comfortable talking to him, Eric?"

"Yes, sure." The Sheffields had lived next door until Jim took his examination for becoming a state policeman. They moved to the other side of town a year ago but the families exchanged visits about once a month.

"When?" Eric asked as he followed Anne and his father to the boat dock.

"I'll call over there when we get home and see if Jim's on duty tomorrow. Is that all right with you?"

"We might as well get it over with," Eric said.

"It may not be as bad as you've thought," his father said. "The right grown-ups could be a help."

"I guess," Eric said. "I *hope.*"

"I was just thinking," Anne said as they walked up to the small booth to pay for using a canoe. "Kids who talk a lot about freedom from grown-ups cause trouble for some of us. And here we are turning to adults."

"Is something wrong about that?" her father asked.

"Some people would say so, I suppose," Anne said. "But I don't think so."

No one mentioned the word *vandalism* or the names *Ron* and *Buffy* the rest of the evening, not until the Markelys were home. The lake was empty except for the ducks, the geese, the swans, and the canoe in which they circled the still water. The moon came up and cast a silver path across the dark surface. The oars made gurgling sounds as they lifted and dipped. Music came softly from the band shell across the drive and over the hill.

"It's nice out here," Anne said as she looked into the sky. "I'm glad we came. I'm glad Mom had this idea."

"She's known for her good ideas," Eric's father said.

4

Eric waited downstairs until his father tried to reach the state policeman by telephone. When no one answered, he decided to go on to bed. Even if Jim Sheffield was contacted that night, they wouldn't get together until the next day or later.

When he went down to breakfast the next morning Eric saw that his mother was shaping ground meat into round mounds. "Hamburgers? For breakfast?" he asked.

"No. We're having a cookout after church with the Sheffields."

"Did Dad talk to them?"

"Yes. There's oatmeal in the orange pan. And

orange juice and milk. Shall I wash my hands and serve you?"

"No, I'm not helpless. Not *that* helpless anyway."

"We'll have to hurry to get to church on time. I let everyone sleep a little longer than I should have this morning."

"Where's Dad? And Anne? Is she up?"

"Your father's reading the *Sunday Star* and Anne's in the backyard talking to Buffy Standish."

"Buffy? She *here?*"

"Yes, she came to the door a half hour or so ago. She asked for Anne. It looked like she'd been crying and her hair was tousled. She used to keep it clean and brushed."

"Not for awhile, she hasn't," Eric said. "Not when I saw her."

Eric was getting up from the table when Anne came into the kitchen. "Mom, would it be terrible if I missed Sunday school today?"

"Why?"

"It's Buffy. She's so scared and upset and doesn't know what to do or where to go. I'm afraid to leave her alone."

"Then you *should* stay with her."

"I know this much," Anne said. "If I felt like she's feeling I'd want someone to stand by me."

"Do you want to invite her inside?"

"Not yet. She's ashamed to face you and Dad. We'll stay in the shelter of the grape arbor until you're gone."

"You aren't afraid to be alone with Buffy and her problems?"

"No, because I've about got her talked into doing what seems to be the right thing. I'd better get

31

back, before she changes her mind and slips away. I'll tell you more later."

When Eric went to his Sunday school class, he saw Tom Raisor. "Hey, I didn't know you were back from vacation."

"I'm not," Tom said. "We came because Mom's cousin or someone is getting married today. Then we'll go back to the lake for another week."

"Do you have to go to the wedding?"

"Mom said I could stay at your house—if you were going to be there, and if you asked, *and*—"

"I *know*. If *my* mom says it's okay. I don't blame you for not wanting to go. Getting all dressed up for a short wedding service isn't worth it to me."

"Me neither."

The teacher came into the room and the boys didn't talk anymore until the class was over. "Come with me to see Mom," Eric said. He was surprised when she didn't agree to invite Tom over at once. Didn't she want Tom to go home with them? Why wouldn't she? Then Eric remembered. The Sheffields were coming for a picnic. But why should that make a difference? They didn't have any children.

He was relieved when his mother turned and said, "Certainly, we'll be glad to have you, Tommy. We've missed you." Eric was sure his mother meant what she said, or she wouldn't have said it. Then he realized that they were going to talk to Jim about Ron breaking the windows. She might think he wouldn't want to talk in front of Tom.

Anne was chopping lettuce into a bowl when Eric followed Tom into the kitchen. Buffy wasn't in sight. "Are you by yourself?" his mother asked.

"Yes," Anne said. "Buffy's gone. I'll tell you more later—a lot."

Does she mean she has a lot to tell or that she'll tell about it a lot later? Eric thought. *Both maybe.*

It was nearly two o'clock before the subject of the brick throwing was mentioned. The paper plates had been burned, the picnic baskets repacked, and the glasses refilled with lemonade. Eric's father called him to the aisle of lawn chairs.

"Something's been going on around here, Tom," Eric said. "We've got to tell Jim Sheffield what we know, Anne and I."

"Maybe I should go somewhere else."

"No, don't. I'd tell you anyway. I can't keep stuff from you. I never could. It's about—well, come on. You'll find out."

"We'd better get this out in the open," Eric's father said. "Jim has to go on patrol at four. Who's to begin?"

Eric took a deep breath and gripped the metal arm of the chair so hard his knuckles were white. "I saw Ron Cranor throw the rocks that broke the church windows. I was in Mrs. Wilton's backyard, behind the lilac bush, trimming grass."

"Are you sure it was the Cranor boy?" Jim Sheffield asked. "Was he alone?"

"No," Eric said. Then he looked at Anne.

"Buffy Standish was with them," Anne said. "She told me so today. She said it was okay to tell you."

"But she didn't throw anything," Eric said. "No one did but Ron. Not there, anyway."

The state policeman asked for the names of

33

others. "I only knew Larry Ross, besides Buffy and a new girl. Her name's Gloria something."

"It wasn't easy for you to tell me this, was it?" Jim Sheffield said.

"Well—that wasn't so bad. But I'm scared of what Ron will do if he finds out."

"There's no need to worry. At least I don't think so. With that many people involved, someone's sure to break down under questioning. They'll tell on each other."

"It's right that this group be caught. I know that," Eric's mother said. "But it's the *why*, the reason for damaging property that concerns me most."

"Vandalism is a problem with many causes," the state policeman said. "That's why the problem's so big, I suppose. Remove one cause, and another produces the same bad results." He went on to say that money is too easy to get. "Earning what you have is not the way many people live. That goes for adults too."

"I know that," Mrs. Sheffield said. "In the classroom I see children who simply won't apply themselves to anything. They expect everything to be easy and fun."

"That may be one of the strongest reasons for vandalism," Jim Sheffield said. "They don't know what they can do, what's good about themselves. Excitement and fun are substitutes for what I call enthusiasm for life."

"I know Buffy feels *she's* not worth anything," Anne said. "No wonder. Her dad and mother tell her over and over how dumb she is. That's what she *says.*"

34

"I'll have to leave in a few minutes," Jim Sheffield said. "Before that, I'd like to ask for your help."

Wow! Eric thought. *Has he changed his mind? Does he want us to testify in court or something?*

"Don't talk about what you know," the policeman said. "Word spreads. Talking about acts of vandalism may give others the same idea, or worse ones."

"You can count on us," Eric's father said. "We don't mean to make matters worse."

"Well, you may or may not hear how this comes out. At least not until the matter's settled."

Tom's parents came a few minutes after the Sheffields left. While their parents talked the boys walked to the driveway. "I bet you were scared when you saw Ron break the window," Tom said.

Eric nodded. "I still am, a little."

"Because of what he'd do if he found out that you saw him? It looks to me like *he's* the one who ought to be scared. I wonder if he is."

"I don't know. Not too much, I guess, or he wouldn't have done it."

"Where's Anne?" Eric asked as Tom and his parents left.

"She had to go. Her Sunday school class is visiting a nursing home this evening. They want to read to the old people and help them write letters— things like that."

"Then we won't know what Buffy told her until later?"

"No, we won't. And for my part I'd like to think about something else for a change," Eric's father said. "How about a game of tennis?"

35

"Great," Eric said. "Where will we go? To school or the city courts?"

"School's closer—if they put the nets up today. *Or* if someone hasn't torn *them* down."

Two girls were on one court. The air was still and the thumping sound of the bouncing ball and the soft beating of running feet on the clay were a little like music. The sun was behind the trees when Eric and his father started home. It left a flush of orange in the gray-blue sky.

"You're getting some power into your volleys," Eric's father said.

"Surprised you, huh?"

"No, not exactly. I've seen improvement all along. As they say—"

"I *know*. Practice makes perfect."

"If not perfect—better. I just thought, does Ron Cranor ever play tennis?"

"Not that I ever saw. Why?"

"He'd be better off if he had something to do. Tennis may not be constructive, but at least it's not destructive."

"I guess he could play if he wanted to," Eric said.

"True. Hey, I've worked off some of the calories I took in at noon. Do you want to stop at the Dairy Dream?"

"Sure."

They sat on a wooden bench at the side of the drive-in and ate their pineapple and caramel sundaes. Business was brisk. Some people came in cars, others rode bikes or motorcycles, and a few walked from nearby houses.

"Oh, man," Eric said after he'd turned to see what was making a sputtering roar.

"What's wrong?"

"There's Ron Cranor on a motorcycle."

"Is he old enough to have a license?"

"No, but that wouldn't stop *him.*"

"Don't be too sure. That's why we have laws, to protect us from the Rons, and those like him from themselves. And sometimes the laws work as they're supposed to do."

5

Eric was restless after Tom left. *It's like that a lot on Sunday evenings. The world seems a little lonely. It could be worse because Tom's family is away these weeks. But even when he's in town I'm glad when Monday comes and I get back to doing usual things. Free time's not so good—at least not too much of it.*

No one was hungry, so Eric's mother said they could help themselves to leftovers. "Thanks for giving your cook a vacation," she said.

"Shouldn't Anne be back by now?" Eric's father asked as he sat down in his rust leather chair and picked up a book.

"Oh, she called and asked to stay with Linda until eight," Mrs. Markely explained. "I felt it would be good for her. She's been so worried about Buffy. Linda will lift her spirits if anyone can."

"So! We'll not know what Buffy told her for awhile longer," Eric's father said.

"No. And I'm not going to question Anne. She'll tell us when she's ready."

Eric was on the way upstairs when his aunt, uncle, and cousins came in the back door. He hurried down to meet the twins, who were also in the eighth grade. "Hi! I was wishing someone would come."

"Here we are," Kent said.

"Yeah, a pair of us," Kurt added.

"What's the matter with your eye, Kent?" Eric asked. "Were you in a fight?" As soon as he'd said the words Eric wished he could grab them back before they reached his cousin's ears. Kent wasn't the kind of person who fought. He was the quiet twin.

"I ran into something, in a way," Kent said. "A boxing glove actually. Some neighbors talked me into learning to spar. I didn't want to, really, but I wasn't brave enough to back out. I just stood there trying to protect myself, and you can see I didn't do a very good job of that."

"Are you mad at whoever it was who punched you?" Eric asked.

"No, just at myself for letting them talk me into something that's a waste of time—actually even stupid of me. What kind of sport is it to try to knock each other's heads off?"

"Want to go to my room or outside?" Eric asked.

"Well," Kurt said, "we brought our racquets. We were wondering if there's a lighted court somewhere close."

"Not at school," Eric answered. "But there's one at Westside Park four blocks away."

Their parents gave the boys permission to go, and promised that someone would pick them up in an hour.

"We keep trying to get Dad to make a court on the other side of our garden," Kurt said.

"That'd be great," Eric said. "Do you think he will?"

"He's been reading books on how to build one. He's not so busy with farm work right now," Kent said. "Say, why don't you come along home with us? School's going to start in two weeks. There's not much time and you haven't been out all summer, except for a couple Saturday nights. Will you ask if you can?"

"I'd like to, but it'd be better to wait a week. I have three yards to mow and I help Dad on Saturdays and sometimes in between."

"How would it be any different in a week?"

"Tom will be back in town. He takes over for me. Like I'm doing his dog exercising for him—a lady's Dalmatian."

"Isn't there anyone else you can get?" Kurt asked.

"I can't think of anyone who'd want to."

"Don't they want money for things?"

"Oh, sure. But a lot of kids get plenty of money without working—from their folks or some way."

"Must be nice!" Kurt said.

"Sometimes I'm not so sure," Eric said. "Hey, we're in luck. Only one court's being used." The boys decided to play sets of only three games, to give each an equal amount of time. Eric was taking his turn at sitting on the bench when he heard the splutter and roar of a motorcycle. Or was there more than one over on the next street. *If that's Ron or anyone looking for trouble, I hope they stay over there, or even farther away,* Eric thought. As he listened, the sound of a siren came from the south. The roar of the motorcyles faded away as the whine of the siren came closer. Was Ron being hunted and chased?

Eric looked up at the sky. A few stars were scattered in the dark blue dome. The quarter moon was a pale gold arc. As he watched, a smoke-like cloud crept across and hid it. Then the music of chimes came from the bell tower of the church. Picures of the boarded-up windows flashed into Eric's mind. He thought of the people who had designed the arched panes, arranging pieces of glass into the form of the Good Shepherd, with lambs resting at His feet. How long had it taken? How many hours had they worked? *It just isn't fair to think that what they took such a long time to finish was destroyed the minute Ron threw those pieces of brick. Why would anyone want to break church windows, or anybody's windows?*

Anne came with her father and uncle to pick up the boys. She ran ahead and told the boys, "I coaxed Dad into letting me play a couple of games. Who's ready to be beaten by a girl?"

"I'm willing to let a girl *try,*" Kurt said.

Kent and Eric sat with their fathers, not saying much. Both wanted to hear what was being said on the subject of building a tennis court. "I'd like to

41

give a hand," Jeremy Markely said. "May be we could come out after work some Saturdays. Meanwhile, I'll talk to Will Raines. He keeps these in shape."

"Dad," Eric said, "the twins asked me to go along home with them this week. But I said next week would suit better when Tom's to substitute for me."

"Well, that may work out. We could take you and maybe we could work together on the new court a while. We'll talk to your mothers."

It was nine-thirty before Eric went upstairs. He waited around for a few minutes for a sign that Anne was ready to talk about Buffy's problem. But his sister said, "I just *have* to wash my hair tonight. My candy-striper hours are from eight-thirty until twelve tomorrow." She wouldn't be out from under the dryer for about an hour. He didn't want to wait up that long. In fact he didn't think he could stay awake even if he tried.

By the time he'd taken a shower Eric wasn't nearly as sleepy as he'd been on the way to his room. He turned on the radio just as the ten o'clock news broadcast began. He stretched out and clasped his hands behind his head. He didn't pay close attention to the newsman until he heard the word *vandalism.* He reached over and turned the volume louder. "One arrest has been made in the case of the broken windows in the Christ United Church. Since the suspect is under sixteen years of age, the name cannot be released. The investigation will continue."

Did they pick Ron up tonight? Eric wondered. *Is that what was happening when I heard the sirens?*

He tried to imagine how he'd feel if he were in Ron's place. *Is he scared, or mad, or sorry—or maybe a little of all three? Is he in jail? Or would his folks get him out some way?* He turned the knob to get music on an FM station. *I've heard enough bad news.* He wished he'd gone home with his cousins. *I'd be farther away from this whole mess.*

"You asleep?" his father asked from the doorway.

"No, just thinking."

"You heard the ten o'clock news?"

"I heard."

"Want to talk?" his father asked. "About how you're feeling?"

"Well, I don't *not* want to."

"Do you know what's bothering you most?"

"One thing is how I'd feel if I was arrested. I'm trying to imagine how Ron's feeling."

"I guess we can't know for sure, since we're *not* Ron. My father used to say we'll never know why the other person limps because even if we wear the same shoes, we don't have the same feet."

Eric smiled. "Dad? Did Grandpa *really* say that? Or is it something you made up?"

"Caught on to me, huh? But going back to Ron. He's experiencing the result *he* caused. Don't forget that."

"I know, but he might not be in jail—if that's where he is—if I hadn't told."

"That's a burden on your mind. I understand that. You acted in a responsible way. Ron didn't. He should be the one who suffers and he probably is."

Eric leaned forward, doubled his pillow, and put it behind his back. "I don't feel good about that."

"No. You wouldn't. But keep this in mind. If

these destructive acts are allowed to go on, more and more people will be hurt—in more ways than one—including Ron himself."

"I did think about that."

"I've done a lot of soul-searching myself," his father said. "We've taken the easy way. We've not faced up to the problem of vandalism, saying this is why we have insurance. We've excused ourselves and shirked our responsibility."

Eric tried to remember what someone had said in health class when they were talking about drug abuse. It had something to do with kids solving their own problems. "Is this a job for you and people like you?" he asked. "I mean, should kids depend on adults for help?"

"Listen, Eric. You are growing up into situations we caused. If we who are supposed to be mature have a let discipline and guidance become lax and weak, how can you be expected to deal with the results alone?"

"I guess that makes some sense," Eric said, as his father turned out the light and headed for the stairs.

6

Before Eric opened his eyes the next morning he realized it was the day he'd be mowing Mrs. Wilton's yard. *It's been a week since Ron broke the windows. In some ways it seems like longer, because I've worried.* He opened his eyes and looked toward the window. *The sun's shining. I'd better take that dog walking. She could use some exercise.*

Anne was going out the back door as he walked into the kitchen. "See you, little brother."

"See you Ann with an *e.*"

"Eric," his mother called from the utility room. "You'll find blueberry muffins in the toaster oven. And cereal and—"

45

"*And* orange juice *and* milk."

He could hear the clang of a metal door, then the *swish-slush* of clothes being tumbled in water. "I hear you're going to the country," his mother said from the door.

"Is that okay?"

"Sounds like a good idea to me. In fact, I'm thinking of visiting Lois a few days myself. How would you like that?"

"Why wouldn't I like it?"

"Oh, I don't know. There seems to be a trend toward making parents outcasts—at least by kids a certain age."

"Well, I'm not that old yet, I guess. I'll let you know when I get there. Okay?"

"Okay, but I hope you never do."

Eric liked the way his mother talked, and the way that she listened when Eric had anything to say. She made room in her mind and took time for what he said, even if she didn't always agree. He remembered one snowy evening. Anne and his dad had gone to the market in the shopping center because his mother didn't like driving on slick streets at all.

Eric was lying face down on the family room floor looking at a new magazine. "It came today," his mother said. "I didn't read much, but one ad caught my eye. It's about in the middle." He turned the pages as she watched from a chair at his side. "There it is, a rooster and a rose."

A white rooster with a bright red comb and curling tail feathers was holding a long-stemmed rose in its mouth. Three pieces of deep blue luggage were arranged on the side of the picture and the words "As light as a rooster and a rose" were underneath.

"I don't know when an ad has caught my attention so completely."

"I don't know, Mom," Eric said. "I don't think it's that good."

"Why? It's colorful and catchy."

"Yes. But I know something about chickens. All roosters aren't the same size. So! How heavy or light is that luggage?"

His mother smiled. "You're right. Logically that's true. I was only thinking of the sight and the sound."

As he poured milk over his cereal and listened to the crackling he asked, "Are you and Aunt Lois going to do something special?"

"No. In fact I've not even talked to her about my idea. It's just—well I need to get back to my roots sometimes, back to the country."

"Don't you like to live in Somerset?"

"I wouldn't want to be anywhere else—not if you and Anne and your father were *here*. But I wouldn't object to the idea of building outside of town. However, that's neither here nor there—whatever that means."

Eric didn't know if he liked the idea of moving or not. *Some things might be good, some not so good. It seems like I'm finding out lately that there's more than one way of looking at a lot of things. It gets kind of confusing.*

The telephone rang as Eric was leaving to go to Mrs. Wilton's. He didn't wait to hear who was calling. *I'm already late. I'll have to put that Lawn Boy into high gear. And myself too.*

47

He was relieved to see that he wouldn't have to do any trimming by hand. *Fortunately, grass doesn't grow as fast under trees and bushes,* he thought. He did stop and rest while he drank the pink lemonade Mrs. Wilton brought to the back door. The slatted swing which hung from the metal frame creaked as it swayed. *This was put here for little kids,* he thought. *Must have been a long time ago.* Bridget, the brown and black beagle, trotted from the front of the house, yipped twice, then lay down on the sun-washed walk of bricks.

"That's a real nice dog you got there," someone said from the alley which ran between Mrs. Wilton's house and the one next door.

Eric turned and saw a tall boy with wire-framed glasses. "It's not mine. I mow this yard."

"Well, anyhow, it's an okay pup. I had one like it. He got hit by a car."

Eric looked sideways at the boy, trying to think where he'd seen him before. Or did he look like someone he already knew? "You live around here?"

"Yeah, in the apartments over on Bundy."

"That's where someone I've heard of lives," Eric said. "I can't think of who right now."

"We just moved there a couple of months ago. I didn't say, but I'm Matt Worden."

"I'm Eric Markely. Well, I'd better get busy. I have another job at noon."

"I wish I could run onto something to do," Matt said. "Maybe if I had—well, I might have got started off better in this town."

Eric and the new boy were together over an hour. They took the dog to the park and talked a lot.

48

"You just moved here—to this town, I mean?"

"Yes, from Richmond—after school was out."

"I'll put this mower away and you can walk with me, if you want—I mean my next job is walking a Dalmatian."

"Okay by me, if it is with you and the dog."

Eric and the new boy in town were together over an hour. They took the dog to the park and talked most of the time. Matt asked questions about the middle school, saying where he'd come from it was still called junior high. Eric said the difference was that the sixth grade was in with seventh and eighth.

Matt mentioned that shortwave radio was his main hobby. "I've fooled around with other stuff, model planes and wood carving and collecting stuff, like campaign buttons and coins. But ham radio— well I don't get tired of it."

"I don't know anyone who does that," Eric said. "It sounds okay."

"I'd like for you to come over and hear the calls. I don't have my license to send. But I have SWL cards from lots of places."

"SWL cards?"

"Yes. We send them to people we hear. They answer sometimes. I heard from an operator way out in Christmas Island in the Pacific. A lot of times you can hear foreign-language broadcasts. SWL means Short Wave Listener."

"That sounds great."

"It sure is. I'd like to have a better set. That's one reason I'd like to get a job."

"If I hear of anything, I can tell you. A lot of kids don't have to work."

"Or wouldn't if they did," Matt said. "I've met a few here and knew more back where we lived."

By the time they returned the black and white dog to its owner, Eric was hungrier than he'd let himself be for a long time. He'd told his mother he wouldn't be home for lunch until one. *Now I don't think I want to wait another half hour.*

He stopped in front of Harvey's Hangout, a drugstore which sold many other things. "Want to go in for a milkshake or ice-cream cone?" he asked. "I'll treat you. I just got paid for two jobs."

"I can pay," Matt said. "But I don't know if I should or not."

Eric wondered why the tall boy kept standing on tiptoe and looking in the wide window. "Does it look crowded?" he asked.

"Sort of. We might have to wait. And I sort of promised someone to be someplace this afternoon."

"That's okay," Eric said. "Can I find your number in the phone book if a job shows up?"

"No, we're unlisted. But I'll copy my number if you have any paper."

Eric felt in his pocket, then looked around. He saw a small yellow bag from Harvey's at the side of the steps. Someone had left a heel mark on one side, so he wrote Matt's number on the other.

"Before I go," Matt said, "do you walk that dog every day? I mean, would it be okay if I came by if I don't have anything to do? If it's not, say so."

"Sure," Eric said. "See you."

When he walked into Harvey's he wondered why Matt thought the place was crowded. One booth was empty and there were two places in the row of stools where they could have sat. *I guess someone*

51

could have gone out the side door while we were talking.

"What will you have?" Harvey asked as Eric looked at the menu and price list above the counter.

"Not much. Just something to keep me going until lunch."

"Your stomach rubbing your backbone?"

"Almost. I've been working. I'll take a medium-size pineapple sundae."

As Harvey spooned the pale gold syrup over two balls of vanilla ice cream, Eric turned on the stool and looked around. He didn't know many people. Most of them were grown-ups eating lunch. Harvey's was that kind of place. Harvey didn't encourage loafing and wouldn't allow loud talk or shoving. Eric remembered the evening when Ron Cranor had been taken by the arm and led to the door.

When Eric turned the other way he saw Larry Ross leaving the second booth. *I guess he's not been picked up. Maybe the police don't know he was with Ron. But it seems that Buffy would have told.*

7

It was three o'clock by the time Eric ate lunch and painted the porch swing for his mother. "You've had a big day," she said as she handed him the can of brush cleaner. "Why don't you do something for fun?"

"I thought I might go swimming. But I'd play tennis if Tom was here."

"Do you want to go to the park pool?"

"No, there's too much rough stuff and klunky talk there. The Y's better. The grown-ups who are supposed to be on the job—well they are, about all the time."

"Do you want me to take you uptown? I'm going

to the library anyway."

"Great! I'd ride my bike, but my legs have had a couple of workouts already."

An hour and a half later Eric's mother was waiting when he came out of the red brick building. She'd said, "I decided it would be better to do my research here. Besides, I don't think there'll be much material I can take home. I'll be reading in periodicals mostly."

"Research on what?"

"On vandalism—its causes." Then she changed the subject to what made the cricket chirping sound in the car engine and the lovely rosebushes in front of the telephone company and the new recipe for cheesecake she was going to try.

Eric saw Anne at the refrigerator when he walked through the back porch. She was still wearing her red-and-white striped uniform. He didn't notice that she wasn't alone until she turned and asked, "Which sounds best, Buffy, lemonade or iced tea? How about you, Eric?"

"I'm not thirsty," Eric said. He was, a little, but he wanted to go to his room. *Or it's more like it to say I don't want to be around Buffy. How do I know how she really feels about my telling on Ron—if she knows? She might be his spy, getting close to Anne to find out all she can.*

"Please don't go upstairs," Anne said. "When Mom comes in we want to talk to both of you. Both of us do."

Eric glanced toward Buffy. She didn't look as if she wanted to talk—not to him or anyone. She looked down at her hands, at one hand twisting the other.

"Where is Mom?"

"She stopped to bring something off the clothes-line. Towels, I think."

"That's my mom," Anne said. "She thinks clothes are cleaner, as she puts it, when they're washed in ozone as well as water."

"Ozone?" Buffy said.

"It's something in the air," Anne explained. "Something that makes clothes smell cleaner."

"That's a switch," Buffy said. "Mostly what's in the air, as far as I know, is real rotten—dirty rotten."

"Oh, Buff! You promised you'd think of better things. Sometimes anyway."

"I'm sorry," Buffy said. "I'm in that kind of grove or rut, I guess. I can't seem to get out of it."

"You could try—harder."

When Eric's mother saw Buffy she smiled and said, "I hoped you'd come back."

"You *did?*"

"Yes. Why don't we go in where it's cooler, if you want to talk to me—or to us."

"I do, Mrs. Markely," Buffy said. "But it's not easy."

"Well, let's see if we can help you."

Anne and Buffy sat at either end of the flowered couch, Eric stretched out in his father's easy chair and his mother sat in her cane-seated rocker.

"Is it Ron you want to talk about?" Ellen Markely asked. "Your involvement with him?"

"That's part of it. But first I'm trying to decide if I should leave home."

"Leave home? Run away?"

"Not run away exactly. No one cares if I'm there

or not. My sister wants me to live with her."

Eric's mother asked if Buffy thought that would be better. She wanted to know if her brother-in-law was in favor of the idea and if money would be a problem.

"I think they really want me. I mean Rosie worries about me. And Hal, that's her husband, gets mad at my folks all the time because of the way they treat me now and how they did Rosie before she got married." She went on to say that her sister had a little boy. "He's so sweet. If I go there Rosie'd take a part-time job at the laundromat, where she worked before. That way I'd be helping out."

"What keeps you from going?" Eric's mother asked. "Are you afraid your parents will try to stop you?"

"No," Buffy said. "It's not that. They wouldn't." Then she began to cry. Tears came first, then choking sobs. She managed to say, "I guess I hate to give up and go. It's hard to admit you're not wanted."

"Do they *say* that?" Eric asked.

"They don't have to *say* it. A person knows. Don't you believe that, Mrs. Markely? That you can know stuff like that?"

"Yes. I believe that," Eric's mother said. "Would it help to think of going to your sister's as a visit? Take a step and see what happens. You might be surprised. You might be happier than you've been for awhile."

"If I was happy, even one little bit, it'd be more than it has been."

Eric began to think the subject of Ron or the window breaking was never going to be mentioned. Buffy quit crying when she told about the room her

56

sister and brother-in-law were fixing for her. "Even though I haven't told them I'll come, they're going right ahead. I think they want to prove to me for sure that they want me to live with them." She said the small room had been a part of a long back porch and had been divided in half. "Hal nailed paneling on the wall, not dark like you see most places. It's pale gray—only I like to call it silver. And Rosie says I could have any color curtains I want. Peach seems pretty."

"It sounds as if you've made up your mind to stay with her," Eric's mother said.

"I guess I have—right now. Everything seems a little better all at once. I think I'll call Rosie. Okay?" After dialing a number and waiting a moment, Buffy said, "The line's busy. I'll try later."

"Perhaps I shouldn't ask," Ellen Markely said, "but how do you feel about Ron Cranor?"

"Not too good," Buffy said. "But mainly I wish I hadn't ever tagged along after him. 'Specially that one day." She said she'd met Ron when he came with Larry Ross to see another boy in the row of apartments where her sister lived. "He was a new kid. Larry had gone to school with this—what's his name—in some other town."

Eric *knew* that she was talking about Matt. *It all fits together. That's where I'd seen him before. He was with Ron and the others. I didn't get as good a look at him because he's taller and I couldn't see his face as well through the lilac bush.*

Buffy brushed her curly, copper-colored bangs back off her forehead. "I guess you already know I was with Ron when he broke the church windows."

"They know," Anne said.

"It's like I told that policeman. I didn't throw any bricks or rocks. No one did, except Ron. Other times Larry did stuff and they tried to get me to—but I didn't."

"Is Ron in jail? When the radio said they caught someone, was it him?" Eric asked.

"It's him all right. I didn't see anyone to ask except the other boy who lives near Rosie. But he said Larry had warned him not to talk. He said he'd really get it when Ron got out."

"Are you afraid?" Ellen Markely asked.

"Yes, some, but not like I was. Besides, I was scared when Ron was breaking things. It wasn't fun—not one bit. And when I'm at Rosie's—I bet I'll feel safer. I think I'll try to call her. Maybe her line won't be busy now."

When Buffy returned from talking to her sister, she was smiling through tears. "She's really glad I made up my mind. And the neatest thing is that when her line was busy she was talking to Mom at the factory. She told mom she wanted me to come, like it was just a visit. She had the same idea you did, Mrs. Markely."

"You going to get clothes from home first?" Anne said. "Could I help?"

"If you want. Rosie's going to be there in twenty minutes in Hal's pickup truck."

After the girls left, Eric's mother said. "It's amazing! That sullen girl was transformed when she turned away from the telephone. It was truly beautiful. I never realized that she had such lovely eyes. You rarely see that shade of violet."

"We didn't find out much about Ron and the other things he's done," Eric said. "Or what's going to happen to him—or the others, including me."

"You?"

"I mean like having to testify or something. I'm kind of a coward, I guess."

"Well, Jim Sheffield said that it probably won't be necessary for you to testify in court. In a way you've already been brave in talking to *him*."

"I guess, but it's scary to think about what Ron may do."

"I read somewhere that real courage is doing the right thing even though you may be afraid at the time. Now I'd better run the sweeper! With people coming, that family room could do with a little cleaning."

"People?"

"Oh, I didn't tell you. The Sheffields and the Porters, and someone they asked, and Bob and Aline Renner, are coming to explore the causes and hopefully find a remedy for vandalism."

What can anyone do? Eric thought.

As if she'd reach his mind his mother said, "It's a big, big problem. And a lot of people would ask what eight or ten people can do. *But* there comes a time when you have to *try.* "

8

The Markelys had hamburgers and stove-top macaroni and cheese for dinner that night. Eric's mother said she'd let them fix their own dessert if they'd like. "We have bananas and apples and there's ice cream in the freezer. I'll have to hurry to get the kitchen in order as it is, what with changing clothes and collecting my thoughts."

"You go on and do what you have to do," Jeremy Markely said. "We'll take KP duty tonight. It shouldn't take three pairs of hands long to clean up this kitchen."

Anne had asked at the table if she and Eric should sit in on the meeting.

"Do you, either of you want to?"

"I don't," Eric said. "I might want to know some of what you talk about, but not everything."

"That's the way I feel," Anne said. "Knowing as much as I do, and being concerned about Buffy, I might say too much."

"What will you do? Go to your rooms or watch TV in the living room?"

"I'm going to write letters, unless you'd like to do something together, Eric," Anne said.

"Like what?"

"Oh, go for a bike ride, or play Monopoly."

"I don't know why, as hard as I've worked, but I'd like to ride for awhile."

"If you leave now," Jeremy Markely said when the kitchen was in order, "you should get home before dark."

"There *are* streetlights, Dad."

"I know, but there are also shadows."

"I never heard you sound afraid before, Dad," Eric said.

"I'm not—for myself."

"Where we going?" Anne asked as they wheeled their bikes over the bumps in the alley.

"Why don't you choose at the first corner, and me at the next. It'll be fun to see where we come out."

Few people were on the sidewalks or in their yards. Two little girls were playing hopscotch at the first corner and another was riding a tricycle. "No wonder kids get by with stuff. No one's around to catch them."

Anne made the last choice before they decided to start home. "Hey!" Eric said. "Did you plan to end up at Harvey's Hangout?"

"Why else did I bring two whole dollars? May I treat you?"

"I could pay. I'm a working guy."

As usual there were only a few empty seats. Eric and Anne sat at one of the small tables between the double row of green plastic booths.

"Harvey's so busy and so are the girls who are helping," Eric said. "I'll go up and get our order. Coke for you?"

"No, orangeade sounds better."

"What kind of a sound does orangeade make, anyway?"

"Go on!" Anne said. "You know what I mean."

As Eric waited at the counter someone said, "You thirsty too?" He turned and saw Matt Worden.

"I didn't know you came over here much. I mean I never saw you in here before."

"Well, I haven't been much—once or twice maybe. And I wasn't sure I wanted to this time. I looked around a little first. But no one I know comes here much."

Eric knew what Matt was thinking. He didn't want to run into Larry or any of the Ron Cranor group. "My sister and I have been bike riding. Do you want to join us at our table?"

"Is it okay?"

"Sure, come on." Eric never felt comfortable about making introductions. He hadn't done it often enough to feel easy. "This is Matt," he said, "and this is Anne. Have a chair."

"Hello," Anne said. "Are you in Eric's class?"

"I keep thinking," Anne said. "But maybe we should go outside before we say more about this."

"Not yet. I've not been in school here. We moved this summer."

"I guess that's why I haven't seen you, if you're new in town."

"Sort of. I live over in the apartments on Bundy Street."

Eric could tell that Anne was putting two and two together and was about to get the right answer.

Matt did the adding for her. "I saw you tonight," he said. "You were helping Buffy Standish move things into her sister's apartment."

"Do you know Buffy?"

"I know her." Matt looked to see if anyone was listening. "We were sort of partners in crime. Man, we were so close to being in deep trouble—it's scary to think about it."

"He was with Ron," Eric said.

"I guessed. Buffy's talked about a new boy."

"Some grown-ups are having a meeting at our house," Eric said, "to talk about ways of cutting down on vandalism."

"Do you think they can?" Matt asked.

"They'll try," Eric said. "My mom will, I know."

"I keep thinking—" Anne said, "But maybe we should go outside before we say more about this." They walked to the corner and sat on one of the benches where people waited to catch buses.

"It's a wonder these seats are still here," Matt said.

"They're chained to the lamppost," Eric said.

"I was going to ask you, Matt, what you think are the reasons for vandalism," Anne said. "I mean, how could it be fun? Like the church windows. Was Ron mad at someone in there?"

"No, I doubt if he knows anyone who goes there, or to any other church."

"Then why would he do it?"

"I can't say about anyone else. But I've listened to Ron talk—a lot—more than enough. He just doesn't care about much, not even himself. I think he scares kids into doing things they shouldn't to make himself feel important."

"Is breaking windows a way of feeling important?" Eric asked.

"No," Matt said, "it's not like that exactly. Ron doesn't get enthusiastic about things—not like I do my shortwave—not anything. He's bored with everything, so he uses excitement as sort of a substitute. He has to keep doing things to make life interesting, maybe."

"That could be," Anne said. "I read something like that, or heard it on TV."

"He ought to get a job or two, like me," Eric said. "I'm almost too tired by night to get into trouble."

"You wouldn't anyway," Anne said.

"Got her fooled, huh?" Matt said. "Say, I'd better go."

"You walking?"

"No, my mom's in a house down the street visiting a cousin. I'll go back there. See you."

Anne and Eric didn't try to talk as they rode home. It wasn't easy for them to hear each other. As they rolled their bikes into the garage, Anne asked, "How did you meet Matt?"

After Eric told where they'd talked that morning, Anne asked, "Do you like him?"

"He's okay. Why? Didn't you get what you call good vibrations?"

"Yes, I did. That's why I was surprised to hear he was one of Ron Cranor's buddies."

"I guess being new makes it hard to know who you want to choose as friends."

"I guess. We don't know so much about that. We've always lived here."

Eric remembered what his mother said about moving to the country. "If we ever *did*, I'd be a new kid."

The meeting was still going on in the family room. Eric took a red apple from the wooden bowl on the cabinet. "I'm going upstairs," he said.

"I will later. I want to call Buffy, and see how she feels about being at her sister's. I'll call from the kitchen."

Eric listened to music on the FM radio until he was sleepy. He thought about what the grown-ups might be saying. He hoped they wouldn't come up with some idea that would be reported in the newspapers. *If names are used, kids like Ron might do worse things to them when he's free just to prove he's tough.* Then a new thought came to Eric. *How do I know they aren't already afraid sometimes—of getting caught or something?*

Anne came to the door. "Are you awake?"

"No, I'm talking in my sleep."

"Okay, okay. I just thought I'd tell you that I talked to Buffy. She sounded happy for the first time since—since we quit being friends."

"You never told me. Why did you quit?"

"Oh, nothing bad like a fight. But Buff wanted to grow up in a big hurry, to wear lipstick and hose and things like that, when they were a bother to me. And you know what Mom always says about hurrying out of childhood."

"I know," Eric said. "Once you've grown up you can't go back."

"Right. Well, I'll see you in the morning. I don't want to get sloppy or anything, but I appreciate you, little brother."

"That shows you're a smart girl!"

9

Eric wasn't sure he hadn't been dreaming until
he sat up in bed the next morning. What could have
been the rumble of trucks was the roll of thunder.
The windowpanes vibrated and a flash of lightning
made them glow for a second. *That means I won't
mow anybody's yard this morning. Even if this is a
shower, the grass will need time to dry.*

He clasped his hands behind his head and looked
at the ceiling. *What can I do with myself today? If
Tom wasn't away he'd help me think of something.*
Then Eric remembered Matt Worden. *I could call
him. I stuck the paper with his phone number in
the W part of my dictionary. Mom says I'm the only*

person she knows who has a Webster filing system.

The smell of frying bacon came up the stairs and led Eric to the kitchen. His father and mother were sitting at the table. "It's almost eight. And you're still here."

"I am at that!" his father said. "It's hard to believe, isn't it?"

"Okay, okay. I just meant that you're usually at the nursery by seven-thirty."

"I wanted to talk to you," Jeremy Markely said, "but hated to drag you out of your warm bed."

Eric reached for the box of rice flakes before he said, "This is about last night, right?"

"No, there's not time to go into that now."

"Besides, we all promised we'd think over what was said, for a day," Eric's mother said. "To get things sorted out in our minds."

"You mean you aren't even going to tell me or Anne?"

"That's not the question. We're going to be busy until evening and the day will end then."

"What am *I* going to be busy at?"

"That's why I waited around," Eric's father said. "To ask if you'd help me out today—for the morning at least." He explained that his ad had been in the paper the day before and he'd been swamped with telephone orders. "I could use two extra pair of hands, as a matter of fact. If Tom was available he'd get a call."

"I know someone who wants a job. At least he says he does." He told about meeting Matt and that he wanted a new shortwave radio. "I don't know if he ever worked with plants before, but I'd show him."

"I'm willing to try him out," Eric's father said. "Do you know how to get hold of him?"

"Sure. I have his number." Eric started to leave the table. He scratched his head and said, "I guess I'd better tell you. Matt was with Ron that day."

"You saw him?" his father asked.

"Not well enough to be sure, but he told me he was. And Anne too. We saw him last night at Harvey's."

"You feel easy about working with him?"

"Sure," Eric said. "He's not like Ron and Larry. He just sort of wandered into the wrong bunch. That's the way I think it was, anyway."

"Like Buffy Standish," Eric's mother said. "She didn't feel that she belonged at home, so she followed anyone who'd accept her."

"I don't think it's bad at home for Matt. He didn't say anything like that. He was new and Ron asked him to go places, so he went."

"It's sad how easy it is for young people to become involved in trouble. It should be as easy for them to go with a good crowd—if it isn't."

"Be careful, Ellen," Eric's father said. "We're not to get into that subject today. Eric, you'd better call your friend."

The telephone buzzed five times and Eric was thinking that Matt was gone when he heard a click, then, "Hello, Worden's."

"Matt?"

"Yes. Who—"

"It's Eric. I was about ready to give up and hang up."

"Well, I had my shortwave headphones on and when I happened to rest my arm on the phone I felt vibrations. What's on your mind? News about Ron maybe?"

"No, I didn't hear anything. Here's why I called. My dad needs someone to help out in the nursery— someone besides me. Want a job?"

"Man, do I! But can I do whatever it is?"

"If I can, you can," Eric said. "After I show you how."

"Should I go over right away?"

"Sure. We're leaving. Got a ride?"

"The bus. It goes close. How about lunch if I'm there that long?"

"You will be. Dad goes out for a box of chicken or cheeseburgers or something."

"Good enough. Thanks, Eric."

The rain had stopped by the time Eric and his father left in the pickup truck. When they came to the second stoplight, Eric looked toward the church. Men were putting boards along the wall where the windows were broken. "They're putting up a scaffold," his father said.

"Will they replace the windows? Will they be like they were before?"

"Not like they were. It'd be hard or even impossible to get stained glass like that. That's a part of the shame of this whole thing."

As the light changed to green Eric saw a boy come from behind the shrubbery under the boarded-up windows. He was carrying a bucket. "Dad, that's Ron Cranor."

"You sure about that?"

"I'm sure. He must be out of jail, but why is he working at the church?"

"I don't know," his father said. "But it makes

sense to me that he'd have to help clean up the mess he made."

By the time Eric had wheeled stacks of pots to the chrysanthemum beds and potted the first flower, Matt was at the door. "So this is what we're to do. You'll have to show me how."

"Sure. All it takes is potting soil, water, and tender loving care. See those roots?"

"Some are almost like hairs."

"I know. That's why we have to be careful. You'll always break some, but the fewer, the better."

Customers came in so often that Matt said, "As soon as we get a table full, someone buys some."

"That's the idea."

"It's like with my mom. She always wants to get a head start when she bakes cookies, so she can keep ahead of me. Only she doesn't do that too often since she went to work at the telephone company. They gave her a job after my dad died."

"When was that?"

"After we got transferred up here. We might go back to Richmond someday."

"Do you want to?"

"It doesn't matter. We've moved a lot. One place is about as good as another. Only this one wasn't too great, until the last two days."

Eric didn't tell Matt about seeing Ron at the church. *He might begin looking worried again. Besides, I don't know for sure how things are. If he asks me if I've heard anything I'll have to tell the truth, but I won't bring up the subject.*

Anne and Buffy Standish came to the potting shed after the boys had worked steadily for over two hours. "What you doing here?" Eric asked.

"Mom sent me for a plant for Mrs. Wilton."

"There it goes again—someone eating our cookies as fast as we bake them," Matt said.

"Cookies?" Buffy and Anne said.

"We'd explain it to you if we thought you'd understand," Eric said.

"Forget it! I think I catch the idea."

"Why's Mom buying Mrs. Wilton a plant? Is it her birthday or something?"

"No, just to make her feel better. Mom wants to cheer her up because of her geraniums."

"*Geraniums?*" Matt and Eric said.

"Yes. Someone upset her stone urns, broke them, and messed up the flowers."

"I guess we can't blame that on Ron," Buffy said.

"I suppose there are others who break things."

Eric scratched his head, forgetting that his finger was coated with moist potting soil. "I don't know who did it," he said. "But it could have been Ron. I mean he might have been out of jail last night. I saw him this morning."

"Oh, man," Matt said. "I hope he leaves me alone."

"Me too," Buffy said. "But you know something. I'm not as scared of him as I was. After all, he can't make me tag along with him. He didn't before. I didn't have to go. I just went."

"I don't want to scare you or anything," Anne said. "What I'm thinking is, will he do something to you if you don't want to be in his group?"

"Could be he'll try," Matt said. "But the way I see it, I've got a choice. This time I know what I'll say."

"We'd better go, Buffy," Anne said. "Which color do you think's prettiest?"

"All of them."

"That's no help!"

"Well, if I was picking, I'd say the lavender and white mixed."

"That's okay by me. Let's go."

Eric's father came to the door a few minutes later. "Why don't you guys take an hour off?"

"And do what?"

"Here's some lunch money if you don't object to walking over to the Burger Chef or the fish food place."

The sun was warm and the sky was blue with only a few puffs of white clouds. "Your dad's okay," Matt said as they waited for a green light before crossing the street.

"Yeah—I think so. We get along on most things."

"So did I with mine. Better than with Mom, until now. She says she was jealous when he took me fishing or on hikes. Now she's ashamed. You know what she said to me last night when I told her about meeting you?"

"Was she mad?"

"No." She cried a little and said she wanted whatever's good for me. Then she told me *she* had a lot of growing up to do after she was married and had me, and that she was still learning."

"Not all grown-ups talk like that, I guess," Eric said.

"No, some think they already know everything."

"And keep saying it over and over."

"You can say that again."

"And over and over and over!"

10

Eric's father came to the potting shed at two-thirty. "I think you're far enough ahead that you can go do something that's more fun."

"I liked this job," Matt said. "It's been a long time since I worked this long. Time went fast."

"Well, since you did good work, I may call on you again," Eric's father said as he paid both boys.

"I'd like that," Matt said. "I mean if you have more than Eric can do. I wouldn't want to push him out."

"Eric, shall I call Mother and ask her to come for you?" his father asked.

"No, I'll ride the bus with Matt."

"You got anything at home to do?" Matt asked as they walked to the bus stop.

"No, not really. Why?"

"I was thinking I might go to see Larry Ross."

"Larry?" Eric was puzzled. *Didn't Matt mean what he said when he wanted to break off from Ron and his group?*

"I just have to get something straight," Matt explained. "It sounds kind of crazy maybe, but this idea came to me when you showed me how to put the chrysanthemums in the pots."

"How, why, what?"

"You said it's better if they're allowed to go straight down as much as possible. If they're tangled or bent they grow a little crooked, and that's not good."

"That's sort of deep thinking," Eric said.

"Well! I've been known to come up with a good idea a time or two."

They took seats in the middle of the bus after looking at the two right behind the driver. They were slashed, one gash crossing another, to make a large cross. Stuffing had begun to escape from the slits. "What happened to the seats?" Eric asked. "Do you know?"

The driver turned his head and said, "Same thing as happens all over town. Kids with nothing to do, and too much money in their pockets, are out looking for excitement. They should have to pay for the damage, when they're caught, or work it off."

Eric thought of Ron.

Is this happening to him? Is he picking up glass today to pay for all the windows he's broken? There's no way he can work them all off on one job.

They'd have to give him work for a long, long time.

When they got off at the stop, which was about halfway between the two boys' homes, Matt asked, "I don't suppose you'd want to come along? I wouldn't if I were in your place."

Eric didn't want to face Larry. He didn't want anything to do with him. *And that's not just because I'm afraid he'll find out I told on Ron. I just don't want to get mixed up with him—no way.*

He scratched his head and a fleck of brown potting soil fell on his T-shirt.

"Like I told you," Matt said, "you're not in this thing. You don't have to go."

"I'm not sure about that. We're all in it in a way, or we soon will be. Seats are slashed, flower urns upset, windows broken. What's next? And who?"

As they turned down a side street, Eric asked Matt how he knew where to look for Larry. "I don't for sure. But often he's with some of his gang on the fire escape in the alley between the secondhand furniture store and the funeral home."

"That's a crazy place to hang out," Eric said.

"I know, and not too comfortable sitting. They used to meet on the library steps, until they were run out because of their klunky language."

By this time Eric was sorry he'd come. Meeting guys like Larry in a dark alley didn't seem too great. *But it's not really dark.*

Matt stopped at the corner of the furniture store. "He's there—alone," he said. "He must be waiting for someone."

"Not for me," Eric said. "I still don't know what you're going to do."

"I—you'll see."

"Hi, Worden. You've been a long time coming around. That's no way for a buddy—"

"I'm not your pal or buddy," Matt said. "That's what I came to tell you—to your face."

"You game to say that to Ron if he comes by?"

"That's what I was wondering. Where is he? You're always glued to him. Or is he in jail?"

"He's out, but the cops—the freaky fuzz—got him on this work kick."

"That's no more than fair," Matt said.

"Man! That's really square-like talk! So what if he broke a window or two? They make new windows every day."

Matt looked up at Larry, who was sitting six steps from the bottom. *Is he going to fight him?* Eric thought. *Up there on those metal steps it'd be real easy to get hurt.*

As Eric watched, Matt went halfway up, stopped, then stooped and picked up the large transistor radio that was on the step below Larry. He held it over his head. "How about me throwing this down on the concrete? It'd make a real loud noise. That'd give us a big kick."

Larry stood up and Matt backed down the steps. "Hey, man. That's mine. I had to work on my folks two whole days to get it."

"So what?" Matt said. "They make them every day. Here, take it."

"You never meant to throw it. You were just putting me on," Larry said.

Matt went halfway up the fire escape, then picked up the large transistor radio that was on the step below Larry.

78

"I didn't mean to throw it. That's right. But I'm serious. It's about time you guys faced up to the truth. Ron talks about facing up but never does it."

"I don't get you."

"You do mean things to other people, but you'd cry like babies if someone did the same things to you." Matt stopped and folded his arms across his chest. "You guys are always yelling about teachers and parents and policemen being unfair. Well, you're worse at that than anyone. You sneak around hurting people who never did one thing to hurt you. And get one more thing straight. Leave me alone. Outlaw me from your group. That's the best thing that you could do for me or any of your old friends now."

Eric had watched Larry's face part of the time. At first he gave Matt sneering looks. Then he began to show puzzled feelings. As Matt said, "Come on, Eric," Larry's mouth was wide open.

"Wow!" Eric said as they reached the sidewalk. "I wouldn't have missed that for anything."

"Surprised you, huh? Well, I surprised myself."

"Would you have said the same thing if Ron had been there?"

"I don't know. I might not have had a chance. They *could* outtalk me."

"You did okay. Great! I wanted to help you out, but you did fine by yourself."

"I know one thing," Matt said. "I feel better."

"Could be that's one thing we all could do more of," Eric said. "Speak out. I think I can from now on without being so scared—now that I heard you."

"Well, here's where I turn off," Matt said. "Do you want to come home with me?"

"Not this time. I had a yard to mow and it rained."

"Are you going to do it now?"

"I'm not sure. I might put it off until tomorrow."

"I'd better go. Mom gets off at four. We're going to a shopping center to buy me some clothes for school."

"I might call you," Eric said.

The house was quiet when Eric reached home. No one was watching TV or listening to a radio. He walked to the foot of the stairs. "Anyone here besides me," he called out.

"I'm here," Anne said as she came to the hall. "Mom's at Mrs. Wilton's."

"Am I supposed to do anything?"

"She didn't say. I'm writing the letters I meant to do last night."

Eric went to the front porch and lay down on the padded swing. He stared at the narrow boards of the ceiling. Why did a lot of people paint them blue? Was there a reason, or did they just copy each other?

It's good to be home, he thought. *But it's not been a bad day.* He wished Tom was home or not so far away that it'd cost a lot to call him. He'd like to tell him about Matt facing Larry.

The swaying of the swing made Eric sleepy. He turned on his side and let his eyelids stay shut. The next thing he knew, even before he opened his eyes, he heard someone come up the three steps from the sidewalk to the porch. He blinked twice, then sat up when he saw that it was the minister. "Hi, I guess I was asleep."

"Don't let me rob you of your rest; I came to talk

81

to your mother about the meeting tonight. Is she at home?"

"I don't know. She wasn't when I came out here. She was at Mrs. Wilton's."

"I see. Then I'll go by there. I want to see her anyway. Anyone who would bother that lady— Well I can't find words to express how I feel about them—not words a preacher should be heard using, anyway."

Eric wondered who was meeting at the church. *I don't remember hearing about any meeting. I guess I'll find out when it's time.*

11

When Eric's father came home, he called from the back door, "Does anyone in there have time to help me?"

"That depends," Ellen Markely said, "on whether you need help more than food. I'm getting dinner, breading tenderloin at the moment."

"That's some choice for a hungry person to make—whether to eat or be a Good Samaritan."

"What do you mean, Dad?" Eric said. "I can help."

"You'll be appreciated. Not that you aren't already." Then Jeremy Markely explained that he'd brought four pots of geraniums for Mrs. Wilton

83

from the greenhouse to replace those the vandals had damaged. He said it was a little late in the summer but it might not frost for awhile and they could be taken inside.

"I thought the urns were broken," Eric said.

"One was and the other had a chip or two out of the base. One of Mrs. Wilton's daughters called. I told her we were in luck. I had one left—one that matches. She said that was one reason her mother was so upset. The urns had been a gift from her children. Said she thought one reason her mother showed people her flowers was so she could tell that her kids bought them for her."

By the time the replacement urn was filled with soil and the geraniums were transplanted, the sun was low and the trees and the lampposts cast long shadows across the sidewalk. Mrs. Wilton watched Eric and his father work and tears filled her eyes as she thanked them for what they were doing for her. "Everyone's been so kind. I don't know when anything's upset me so much. Just to think that Somerset boys, and maybe girls, would do mean things is painful to me. I've lived in this town and loved it for over sixty years—nearly all my life."

"Did you know there's to be a meeting at the church tonight to talk of ways to counteract vandalism?"

"Yes, the minister told me," Mrs. Wilton said. "And I'd like to go in a way. But I hate to walk into my yard alone afterward. Just think of that! Afraid in Somerset. I didn't think we'd ever come to that."

"You don't need to come home alone," Eric's father said. "Or go by yourself either. Ellen and I will be your bodyguards."

Eric was upset as they loaded what was left of the potting soil into the pickup truck and rode the three blocks to his home. Would kids like Ron go as far as hurting someone? Or was Mrs. Wilton uneasy because someone had come into her yard while she was there and messed things up?

At the table the conversation was mainly on the subject of the meeting at the church. "Is it the same group that was here?" Anne asked.

"They've been called," her mother said. "But there will be others—people from the church—because of the broken windows, the expense of replacing them, and Mrs. Wilton's trouble."

"Do you think anything will be done?" Eric asked. "Except talk?"

His father shook his head as he put sour cream on his baked potato. "Is that how it seems to you? That grown-ups only talk about doing things?"

"Well," Eric said, "sometimes it's like that."

"Indeed it is," his mother said. "Many people are willing to talk about doing something but when it comes to action, the number dwindles."

"I've already come up with one idea," Eric's father said. "It seems to me that Mrs. Wilton was afraid, not so much to go to church alone, but more to come back. She no doubt thinks someone could have broken in while she's away—and may still be there."

"She's probably not the only person who has that fear. So many people live alone."

"I guess that's another good thing about families," Anne said. "They're protection."

"They *should* be," her mother said. "But they aren't always."

For the first time in a long while Eric thought about Ron Cranor's family. *Hadn't they known where he was or what he was doing? Didn't they care? How did they feel now?*

"Do you two want to go to the meeting?" Eric's mother asked.

"I think I will," Anne said.

"How about you, Eric?"

"I don't know."

"I'll tell you why I want to be there," Anne said. "In the first place, I don't want to wait until you get home to find out what happened. And in the second place, why shouldn't kids and grown-ups meet and talk together? I mean, we're all involved."

"That's true," her mother said. "And there's this strong tendency to put blame on whoever's not around." She told of going to a meeting in Indianapolis. It was to explore the idea of how parents and teachers could help the schools. Some teachers said homes didn't do all they should. A mother blamed teachers for not doing a good job."

"And what did you say, Ellen?"

"How did you know I said anything?"

"Because I know *you.*"

"Well, I told them, here we are shooting arrows of blame across a kind of no-man's-land. And that's where our children are. They're the ones being hurt."

Anne started to clap her hands, her father stood up and bowed, and Eric grinned. "My mom's not afraid to speak out, or if she is scared, she does it anyway."

As they left the house Eric's mother said, "I find *myself* dreading to come home now. Not that I'm afraid personally, but I keep thinking something here will be damaged. I don't like being suspicious."

"It's a kind of contagion," Eric's father said. "The disease spreads from one mind to others."

Eric was surprised when he walked down the aisle ahead of his father. Matt Worden was sitting at the far end of a seat on the left. "There's Matt. Is it okay if I sit with him?"

"Go ahead."

As Eric slid along the polished wood of the pew, he said, "I never thought you'd be here."

"I figured you'd be surprised." Matt explained that his mother's cousin had told them about the meeting. "We ate out at the cafeteria and she came to meet us. She's two seats ahead with Mom."

"They look alike. Which is your mom?"

"The one with the blue dress."

"They're both pretty. I guess I *have* seen the other one here."

"We might come too. We just never got started anywhere after we moved. You think many people will be here tonight?"

"Doesn't look like it," Eric said. "It's almost seven-thirty."

The minister came to the front, but didn't stand behind the pulpit. "I've called this meeting in a hurry," he said, "but not without some thought. I've contacted people who I know are concerned. This doesn't mean there aren't others. When we hear of their interest, they'll be included—if they wish." He went on to explain that everyone present had either been victims of vandalism or had knowledge of who was involved.

"That's us," Eric whispered.

"That's us."

As the minister asked for suggestions or ideas Eric thought, *Was Matt's mother invited because he was with Ron? Who would have told the preacher? That cousin maybe.*

Two people said they should demand better police protection and another answered that policemen couldn't be everywhere at all times.

A man who said he was a church trustee stood and turned to face the others. "One positive change about vandals has been made. The judge in the case of the individual who broke store windows has given him a choice—either work and pay the damages or go to the state boys' school."

That might not work all the time, Eric thought. *Some guys would get madder and do even worse things.*

"You've discussed the responsibility of the police and proper punishment. How about our part?" the minister asked.

"That's what I've been considering," Eric's mother said. "Prevention might be the best remedy."

"What can we do that we've not already done?" a woman asked. "We've put up bright lights in our backyard, changed locks, and such as that."

"I'm thinking along the lines of shared concerns not only for ourselves but others," Ellen Markely said. "Would all of us speak out or get involved if we saw a stranger in our neighbor's yard?"

Eric began to think that this was another all-talk-and-no-do meeting when his father stood up.

"Let's get practical and do something. We can begin, at least. There are people in this church who don't come to a meeting because they're afraid to go home alone. Can't we do something about *that*, for starters?"

The minister looked at the clock. "I suggest that we choose a committee to come up with ideas—and meet here in a week." Eric's mother, the church trustee, and Mrs. Wilton were nominated and appointed.

Again Eric's father spoke. "We may be overlooking something, a source of understanding. Young people go to this church. Let's contact the teachers of junior and senior high Sunday school classes for a list of young people who would be willing to sit in on our meetings."

I know why Dad did it like that, Eric thought. *We were two thirds of the kids here. He wouldn't want to seem to be choosing Anne and me.*

After they'd seen Mrs. Wilton inside her house and as they walked home Eric's mother said, "Do you realize we're on two committees, working for the same purpose?"

"I don't see any harm in that," Eric's father said, "This is a big problem. It needs a lot of concerned people if anything's to be changed."

12

When Eric opened his eyes the next morning he thought, *Three more days and I'll be out on the farm. Will Mom still go now that there's all this talk about doing something about vandalism?* He blinked his eyes and stretched his arms above his head. *I'm tired of thinking about all this trouble. I'll be glad to get away from talk about it. Besides, I don't see what I can do to help anything.*

Anne was in the kitchen when he went downstairs. "Good morning, Ric. Are you awake? Or just up?"

"Both," Eric said. "Where's Mom?"

"She's over at Mrs. Wilton's checking to see if

things are okay. What are you going to do today?"

"I don't know. The yards are mowed and Dad didn't say anything about needing me."

"I'm going to Buffy's this morning. She stays with her sister's little boy in the afternoon, so we're going swimming before noon. Afterward, this is my day to read at the library Children's Hour. Mom left cooked cereal."

Eric watched a half hour of the morning news on television, and was rolling his bike out of the garage when he met his mother in the alley. "Are you still going to see Aunt Lois?" he asked.

"Yes, but only for two days," she said. "I've decided that's long enough for a visit. But you can stay on. Are you on the way somewhere now or just riding?"

"Riding. I like early mornings."

"So do I," his mother said. "For example, I wonder how many people have really looked at a spider web at this time of day. I stopped at a wire fence on the way home. All the snowy strands were beaded with dew. Only a spider can give the world a sight like that."

Eric rode down the alley and across the boulevard to a side street to get out of the traffic. The sun wasn't high in the sky and the air was still cool. He stirred it into movement as he rode and the breeze brushed his face. He reached Westside Park and took the bike trail to the curve of the river, then turned back. As he crossed one park drive he saw that someone was sitting on a green bench. Whoever it was was looking down at first. When he raised his head, Eric recognized Ron Cranor.

What will I do? What will he do? Eric wondered

91

as he coasted toward Ron. He had recognized Ron too late to avoid him without being rude.

Without thinking, without understanding why, Eric braked the bike and stopped a few feet away. "You okay?"

Ron nodded.

"Well, I thought maybe—"

Eric realized that he didn't know what he'd thought. He saw Ron, stopped, and that's all there was to it. *I guess it was a dumb idea.* He was ready to go on when Ron said, "I didn't think you'd have anything to do with me."

Eric couldn't ask why. He knew. "You mean because you're in trouble?"

"Yeah. I *thought* you'd know. Everybody in the whole town probably knows."

"Maybe not. I mean a lot of people don't pay much attention to what goes on." Eric's throat began to feel tight. What if Ron asked him how he knew? *I'm not brave enough to say I saw him break the windows. Will I ever be? Or would it help any if I did? I don't know. Some thing's are hard to figure out.*

"I suppose you're wondering if I learned my lesson?" Ron asked.

"No, I guess that's your business."

"I guess. Maybe I have. Maybe I haven't."

Eric wanted to ask what he was doing, sitting all by himself out in the park. *It seems funny—kind of odd. He always had kids tagging along after him.*

"Well, there's my ride. I gotta go," Ron said. He

Without thinking, without understanding why, Eric braked the bike and stopped a few feet away.

walked across the grass and the bike trail over to the driveway. A red pickup truck stopped and he climbed in, glancing at Eric as he rode away.

That might be someone he has to work for, Eric thought. All the way home Ron's face was in Eric's mind. *He didn't look mad, not like I thought he'd be. A little sad, maybe, but mostly like nothing mattered. I guess that is sad, though.*

"Matt called," Eric's mother said as he wheeled his bike into the yard. She was pulling weeds from around her cannas. "This peat moss was supposed to keep weeds down, but some poked through anyway."

"Did Matt say what he wanted?"

"No, I didn't ask. Even if I'd have asked, 'May I take a message,' I'd have sounded too curious to myself. You're to call him."

"Are you doing anything today?" Matt asked.

"No, no jobs. Why?"

"Well, I told my mom I'd go to the shopping center and get a new lock for our door. Do you want to go along on the bus?"

"Sure. If Mom says it's okay. When? Where'll I meet you?"

"I can't go until after lunch, because I'm helping Buffy's sister. She's making a playpen for her little boy."

"Are you sure you're not helping Buffy?"

"No, she's not home."

"That's right. She went swimming with Anne."

When Eric asked if he could go with Matt, his mother said, "I'd thought of going to the mall myself. You could ride along. Why don't you see if Matt wants us to go by his home? It's on the way."

The boys waited for Eric's mother while she shopped in the food market. "I saw Ron this morning," Eric said. "I hadn't thought to tell you."

Matt listened as Eric told about the conversation in the park. "I had the feeling that he doesn't care much about the trouble he's in."

"That's nothing new."

"What do you mean?"

"That's the way he is," Matt said. "Nothing means anything to him, unless it's bossing kids around." He ran a finger along the dashboard, back and forth, back and forth. "Lately I've been thinking that Ron—well, that he doesn't mean much to himself." Matt explained that Ron didn't make good grades. "I guess you already know that. He's in your grade, isn't he?"

"No, I've never been in the same class with him. Ron failed twice."

"Well, he fails in a lot of ways. I've heard him say he's one of the dumb ones. He says it like he's bragging, only I don't think he is."

"It looked to me like he was getting a kick out of throwing that brick that day."

"Maybe, like I said, he was looking for excitement—to keep from being bored."

"Maybe," Eric said. "There's Mom."

The boys helped put the brown bags into the car trunk. As Eric slammed the lid so it would latch, his mother said, "How would you boys react if I offered to treat you to a—to something at the drive-in?"

"How about it, Matt?"

"Why would I say no? Thanks, Mrs. Markely."

When they drove in, Eric's mother bypassed the

plastic canopy. "Let's go inside where it's cooler."

"I've never been here," Matt said as they took their brown trays to an orange booth. "But there are plenty of places like that in this town."

"You're new here, aren't you?" Eric's mother asked.

"Sort of."

"I've not always lived here either. But I have been in Somerset long enough to feel in place."

They talked as they ate. Matt told a little about other places where he'd lived, and the names of schools he could remember.

"Did you always want to move?" Eric asked.

"I *never* wanted to. I'd get mad when I was little and cry. After I was in school it was worse. Once I thought I'd hit back at my dad and mom. I didn't try in school and almost failed on purpose. I did that so they'd feel bad for making me leave my friends in Waldon—I *think* it was Waldon. That's funny-peculiar. I remember being mad about leaving, but am not sure which school it was. Could be that's because I didn't want to leave any of them."

"I hope you like Somerset School," Eric's mother said, "and that the bad experiences of this summer won't give you a bad feeling."

Matt stirred the crushed ice in the tall cup with the orange and white striped straw. "There's good here too. Now there is."

"I've been thinking all morning that I'd like for you and your mother to come over and eat with us tonight. Perhaps we could have a cookout."

"Do you know her?"

"Yes, we talked for a few minutes at the church meeting. Can you give me her number at work?"

96

"Do you think she'll come?" Eric asked Matt.

"I think—I hope—so. She doesn't go out much. She only knows people at work mostly."

As Matt got out of the car, Eric's mother said, "Either your mother or I will let you know about tonight."

On the way home she said, "I like Matt. He looks at me with such honesty. It's hard to believe he was involved with Ron."

"He really wasn't. He just came close," Eric said. He told about the meeting with Larry on the fire escape. "Matt stood right up to Larry. I think he's a lot braver than I am."

"Why do you say that?"

"Well, I didn't tell anyone what I saw—not at first. I was scared then, and I still was when we went down that alley. And even this morning when I talked to Ron—I guess I didn't tell you about that."

After he finished telling her, his mother said, "Remember, you did tell, you did go with Matt, and you did stop and treat Ron with kindness."

"I don't know about the kindness part. I just stopped."

Ellen Markely called to invite Matt and his mother for a cookout. Eric heard her say. "I'm sorry. Could you make it tomorrow? Fine! About six then."

As she turned from the telephone she said, "Mrs. Worden is working overtime tonight."

13

Anne came down the stairs from her room as Eric started toward his. "You people!" she said. "I've tried all day to get you—when I wasn't doing something else. Haven't you been at home at all?"

"Yes," her mother said, "in and out. Did you need something? You could have called your father."

"I did—to find out where you could be. He didn't know. He said he couldn't keep track of all of us and that he was the one who stays put—more or less."

"Was there a problem?"

"No, but there could have been. I mean my heart was pounding. I didn't know what was going to happen next."

Eric sat down on the third from the bottom step. "You might as well find a chair, Mom, until she gets to the point."

"Yes, Anne, what *are* you talking about? And whatever it is, you'll have to come to the kitchen. I have groceries to put away and a meal to cook."

Anne leaned against the birch cabinets and talked until the brown bags were empty. Sometimes she was asked to move while Eric and her mother put cans or boxes in drawers or on shelves. "It all happened as we left the pool. Outside the wire gate Ron Cranor came up to Buffy. He didn't even look at me. Anyway, right off he said, 'Were you the one who ratted on me, Buff?' "

Anne said that Buffy's face turned red, then white around her mouth. "I could tell that she wanted to run. So did I. But Buffy stood and looked at Ron then she said, 'I told the truth when I was asked. I didn't go to anyone, but maybe I should have.' "

"Did Ron get mad?"

"I don't know," Anne said. "We couldn't tell by the look on his face or the sound of his voice."

Eric listened as Anne told about the two-sided conversation. "I never said a word. The longer they talked, the more Buffy said. Ron got sort of squeezed out." She remembered that Buffy had said that going out and breaking stuff was stupid. "She put it this way, 'You act like you're going to make a career of it or something—and that being a vandal takes some special training. That's *dumb.*' "

"Looks like Ron would have got mad then," Eric said.

"He didn't. He just stood there wiggling a foot

back and forth on the walk. But before we left, he made a kind of threat."

"Threat!"

"Yes. He asked how she'd feel if a brick went through her window. 'It could,' he added. His ears got red then."

"What did Buffy say to that?" Eric's mother said.

"She walked closer to Ron and told him he should know better than to hit back at her. 'You'll be the first one they'd suspect now. You've done that to yourself.'"

"That's right," Eric's mother said. "It's so sad to think the boy has a record because of one incident."

"Buffy talked as if there'd been other times when Ron was caught. She said he bragged about it anyway."

"Bragged?" Eric said.

"That's the way it came out."

"Do you think Ron will do bad things to Buffy's family?" Eric asked.

"She said she wasn't afraid. That's the last thing she said to Ron. 'You don't scare me. You don't do things out in the open. You sneak down alleys and creep around in the dark.'"

"Wow," Eric said, "she's really brave."

"Yes she is," his mother agreed. "And some of us could learn by taking lessons from her."

"What do you mean?" Anne asked.

"I don't know—not exactly. Just that it's time for plain speaking, for strong action. Buffy and Matt, who were in Ron's group, were brave and faced him. We grown-ups surely can do as much or more. Oh, look at the time! I must get the potatoes scrubbed and into the oven!"

100

"I'll do that, Mom," Eric said, "unless that will make Anne mad."

"Go ahead. Be my guest."

"I have an errand for you, Anne. I bought some extra white grapes. Mrs. Wilton loves them. Will you take them over?"

"Mom!" Anne said. "You just want to see if she's all right—to check on her."

"Anything wrong with that?"

After Anne left, neither Eric nor his mother spoke for several minutes. He'd put the fourth foil-wrapped potato in the oven before he said, "Ron still doesn't know I told on him."

"That still worries you, doesn't it?"

"Some."

"That's part of accepting responsibility, I suppose—part of the consequences."

"It seems sort of heavy—kind of a load."

"I know. But the longer you go without Ron finding out, the less you'll worry. That's the way it seems. Time takes care of things."

"That's better than Ron taking care of me. But you know something, Mom? I'm not proud of being afraid."

"Listen, Eric, like I told you before, doing the right thing even though you're afraid takes courage."

Eric shook his head. "I'll have to think about that, I guess."

Jim Sheffield came to the door while the Markelys were still at the table. "I can't stay long, but I wanted to tell you what happened today. I was at the noon meeting of my service club. We had a round-table discussion on vandalism. We came up with a move which may make it harder for people to get by with breaking and damaging other people's things."

The idea, as Jim explained, was to involve various neighborhoods. He had talked to a man who'd been paying to work out in a gym. "And he came up with the suggestion that others join him in jogging, or riding bikes, or walking together in their parts of town."

"I see the value in that," Jeremy Markely said. "Too many of us either hide behind a newspaper or are glued to the TV or try to get out of town every chance we get. We leave the coast clear for trouble-makers."

"Right. Under our new plan some of us will be monitors on our streets. I thought maybe we could bring this up when we meet again. And I'm supposed to ask, Is tomorrow night clear for you?"

Eric's mother nodded and his father said, "We'll be there."

After Jim left, Anne said, "I can see that grown-ups being around might keep kids from tearing up stuff. But some—well, they may think they're being spies."

"Could be," her father said. "But if it helps, does that matter? I learned long ago that to have some people say bad things about you is compliment."

"How could that be?" Eric asked.

"Simple. If they think wrong is okay, they'll think an okay guy is bad. Understand?"

"I'm not sure. I'll think about it."

The telephone rang four times before bedtime. Two calls were for Anne and two for her mother. Eric was on the floor trying to hold his eyelids open until the end of a baseball game on TV, when the fifth call came. "It's for you, Ric," Anne said. "It's Tom."

Eric stumbled over a pillow and bumped into a chair. *I must have been nearly asleep.*

"Hi! I thought you were staying until Saturday."

"No, it rained a lot up there. What's going on? Same stuff, huh."

"Well, no," Eric said. He thought back a week. "A lot happened."

"Good or bad?"

"Well, good mostly." Eric didn't really want to talk the whole thing over. *For one thing, I'm tired. And I'd like to forget all this for awhile.* So he said, "It's mostly about Ron Cranor and his group."

"Real rough bunch, huh?" Tom said.

"Not all of them. I'll tell you more tomorrow. Okay?"

"Okay. My mom said I wasn't to stay on the phone. She has to call my grandmother and aunt to tell them we're home. She'll probably say a lot more than that. You busy in the morning?"

"Not very. See you."

"I'm going to bed, Mom," Eric called. "I'm walking and talking in my sleep."

As he showered, he wondered if Tom would like Matt. *I think he will. And we never get mad if the other person makes a new friend.* He thought of the next week when he'd be at the farm. *I mustn't forget to write down whose yards Tom will have to mow. And that Mrs. Wilton's grass may need to be clipped around the trees. I guess if Tom has other stuff to do he wouldn't care if Matt took over one job. I'll find out—tomorrow.*

Getting ready for bed made Eric feel less sleepy.

103

He turned on the FM radio. That made him think of Matt's shortwave radio. *I didn't get over to listen with him. That sounds like a good hobby. Maybe I could take it up someday. I could start by getting some of those SWL cards printed with my name on them. I'll have to ask how much they cost.*

Eric was reaching for the switch on the radio when his father came to the door. "Can you postpone sleep a minute or two?"

"I'll try. Why? Something wrong?"

"Oh, no, but your mother told me you'd put yourself down for being scared."

"Well, I'm sort of over that—on account of what she said. But if Ron hears—then—who knows how I'll feel?"

"Let me ask you this? If you had it to do over, would you tell that you saw Ron throw the brick?"

Eric took a deep breath. "Yes, I'd have to. Even if I didn't know anything would get better, I'd have to tell."

"That's what I thought you'd say. And I believe you're right."

14

The next day Eric's family was busy getting ready to leave. Aunt Lois called and insisted that the Markely family come out early enough on Sunday to go to church with them. After some discussion all four agreed to leave Somerset at eight o'clock.

"I'd really like to go to church out there," Ellen said. "I'll enjoy meeting some of Mama's friends and mine again, those who haven't moved away."

"I'll have to tell Tom whose yard to mow and stuff like that," Eric said. "I'll be at the nursery all day tomorrow."

"I've been thinking of calling Matt," his father

said. "There's a lot of transplanting left to do and I have seven deliveries to make, as of right now. You can help a little today if you wish and get off earlier tomorrow."

"Okay, I'll be there after I see Tom."

"Anne," her mother said, "are you sure you'll not be afraid or feel neglected? I don't like leaving you even though you did volunteer to cook for your father."

"Mom! I volunteered to be a candy-striper. And I'll *be* here." She went on to say that several girls were on vacation and others had to put in extra time. "I tell you what I would like to do. May I have Buffy over if she doesn't have to babysit?"

Eric looked at his mother. Her forehead wrinkled into a frown. *She's thinking Ron might come here—to hurt Buffy.*

"Don't you want her here?" Anne asked.

"Certainly. I just had to rise above the feeling of fear that the thought of Ron brings to my mind."

"We'll be okay," Anne said. "Dad will be here. And you're going to be gone only two days."

"Well, I must get busy. I still have to shop for our cookout, clean the house, and make phone calls for tomorrow night's meeting."

"I'll do the upstairs," Anne said. "I'm not due at the hospital until eleven."

"Every little bit of help will be appreciated."

"How would it be if I watered the flower boxes?" Eric asked. "The moss rose is droopy."

As he was pulling the hose around the corner of the house, Tom came across the yard. They talked as Eric worked—about Ron being made to work to pay for damages, about Buffy and Matt standing up to Ron, and what people were trying to do to cut down on vandalism.

"I know one thing I can do," Tom said. "I started already."

"Started what?"

"Well, I was on the way over here and Larry Ross was coming down the alley. I didn't want to stop, but he got off his bike and waited on me."

"What did he want?"

"To blow off about things he'd done. He said, 'You've been gone so you don't know. Man, you ought to have heard that glass break when old Ron crashed it. Out of sight!' "

"What did you say?"

"Well, I didn't want to say anything, but I did. First I told him, 'Big deal. How hard is it to hit big wide windows! What's so great about that?' "

"What did Larry say?"

"Nothing. He just stood there. He didn't know what to say, I guess. He wasn't impressing me."

"So it wasn't any fun," Eric said. "Maybe that's one thing all of us can do when they talk big. We can say, 'So what?' "

"I felt good when Larry went on down the alley— better than when I just listened. What you going to do this afternoon?"

"Help Dad. Why?"

"I thought I might go swimming."

"Well, before I leave for the farm I'll write down where you can mow—if you still want to do it. If you get a chance to do something else, Matt Worden will help out."

"That makes me think of something Larry said about Matt. He called him a chicken."

"He's not—not one bit."

"Anyway, I said, 'How'd you know he's a chicken? Did he have feathers, lay an egg, or go cock-a-doodle-doo?' "

"That's a good answer," Eric said. "I'm going to remember that. Did Larry say anything back to you?"

"No, he didn't know what to say. I'd better let you go. Have fun at the farm."

"Thanks. By the time I get back it'll be time for school to start."

"I sure hope things quiet down before then," Tom said.

"I think they have already—some anyway."

Eric put the hose away, and ate a lunch of cream of tomato soup and ham salad sandwiches before going to the nursery. "I'm covered up with work," his father said. "I called Matt to help dig me out. He'll go home with us."

The boys had little time to talk until evening. Eric stayed in the salesroom while Matt potted plants. During a break Eric walked to the door and said, "You getting along okay?"

"Great," Matt said. "I've got a system. I line up the pots, fill them with soil, then go down the row with the clumps of plants."

On the way home Jeremy Markely said, "In case I forget, Matt, call me about nine every morning next week. By that time I'll see how the day's going. If you're free and I need help, you're hired. I'd better take advantage of good help before school starts."

Matt's mother was in the backyard turning ground meat patties on the wire grill when they walked through the garage. "Ellen's put you to work, I see," Jeremy Markely said.

"After I insisted. You all right, Matthew?"

"Sure."

"Hasn't he complained because I'm a slave driver?"

"No, indeed. He's grateful. And so am I—for so much."

Eric could see tears in Mrs. Worden's eyes. *She's glad Matt didn't get in trouble.*

The pale moon was high in the sky before Matt and his mother mentioned going home. "We could move inside," Ellen Markely said as they cleared the picnic table.

"It's nice out here," Mrs. Worden said. "We won't have many more nights this warm."

Eric's father put more wood in the stone fireplace. Sparks danced in the air and faded into the darkness. Smoke curled from the square chimney. The conversation wandered from one subject to another. Mrs. Worden said that a full moon always reminded her of the year they'd live on a houseboat. "I loved watching the moon come up and cast a path of light across the river."

"Was that fun for you, Matt?" Eric asked.

"Matt wasn't born," Mrs. Worden said. "I would have been afraid he'd fall overboard. Later would have been fine. But by then we'd been transferred at least seven times."

"Is there someplace you'd rather live—of all the places you've been?"

"No, not really. If I have a choice, which I pretty much have, I'll stay here now that Matthew's more settled."

After the Wordens left, Anne said, "I'm a little chilly."

"Perhaps we'd better go in," her mother said. "By the way, Anne, you were quiet tonight—unusually so. Are you all right?"

"I'm fine. I like to listen to people talk. Mrs. Arless says that's why I'm a good candy-striper. I listen to people. Sometimes they make me sad or upset, but I listen."

"I want to talk to you and to Eric," her father said. "We'll all be at a meeting tomorrow night and we'll not be together for a week."

What's he going to say? Eric thought. *Has he heard something? Like me having to testify or something?*

"Let's go in the family room," Ellen Markely said. "We've had a busy day and might as well be comfortable. Or does this involve me?"

"Yes, it involves you. You're the mother of these two. Am I right about that?"

"You're right. I confess—with pride, I might say."

This must not be serious. Dad's teasing.

Eric didn't sit all the way back on the end of the couch. He ran a finger up and down the wood part of the arm while he waited to hear what his father wanted to say.

"We've come up with a lot of ideas on how to curb vandalism and I think they'll do some good. We'll not get rid of it altogether, but we can help do what people call 'reverse the trend.' But I think we've overlooked and failed to give credit for one of the most positive moves. The one made by the Markely kids."

110

Eric looked at Anne. She raised her eyebrows and shrugged her shoulders.

"Is there something *I* don't know?" Ellen Markely said.

"You know. But unless you're different from me you may not have appreciated what Anne and Eric have done—for Buffy and Matt."

"For Buffy and Matt?"

"What did we do?" Anne asked.

"You offered them friendship—something better than the Cranor boy had given. Not everyone would have done that."

"Why, Dad?" Anne asked. "Oh, maybe I do know what you mean—that we could have put them down."

"Yes. And made it easier to keep on with Ron's ways."

"Well," Anne said, "I couldn't do that. You see, I knew Buffy before. I knew how she used to be long ago, when she wasn't so unhappy at home."

"It was the other way with Matt and me," Eric said. "I didn't know him before, and I didn't know he'd been with Ron that day—not at first. He began talking to me and I thought he was okay."

"The key words may be 'offered them something better,'" Eric's mother said. "The world could use a lot of that."

"No matter what you say," Jeremy Markely said, "you showed a special kind of feeling—compassion, you might say."

"I never thought of it that way," Anne said. "I just did what seemed right—maybe what I might want someone to do for me. How about you, Ric?"

"Same here."

111

Dorothy Hamilton, a Selma, Indiana, housewife began writing books after she became a grandmother. As a private tutor, she has helped hundreds of students with learning difficulties. Many of her books reflect the hurts she observed in her students. She offers hope to others in similar circumstances.

Mindy is caught in the middle of her parents' divorce. *Charco* and his family live on unemployment checks. *Jason* would like to attend a trade school, but his parents want him to go to college.

Other titles include: *Anita's Choice* (migrant workers), *Bittersweet Days* (snobbery at school), *The Blue Caboose* (less expensive housing), *Busboys at Big Bend* (Mexican-American friendship), *The Castle* (friendship), *Christmas for Holly* (a foster child), *Cricket* (a pony story), *Eric's Discovery* (vandalism), and *The Gift of a Home* (problems of becoming rich).

Mrs. Hamilton is also author of *Jim Musco* (a Delaware Indian boy), *Ken's Hideout* (his father died), *Kerry* (growing up), *Linda's Rain Tree* (a black girl), *Mari's Mountain* (a runaway girl), *Neva's Patchwork Pillow* (Appalachia), *Rosalie* (life in Grandma's day), *Straight Mark* (drugs), *Tony Savala* (a Basque boy), and *Winter Girl* (jealousy).